FINDING LOVE IN ALASKA

Perfectly
MOOSEMATCHED

Copy Editor: Write Girl Editing Services

Cover Design: Alt 19 Creative

Proofreading: FictionEdit.com

Chapter One

SADIE

Dodging family dinner undetected was tricky enough without a giant moose posing as a roadblock. Sadie Evans' heart pounded against her rib cage as she froze in place. The sheer size of the four-legged obstacle with massive antlers was intimidating enough. But put said beast a mere seven or eight feet in front of her sandaled feet, and she only had space enough in her panicked brain to hope the moose didn't decide to toss her around like a ragdoll.

"Ed, this is *really* bad timing," she hissed. To be fair, had she known the notorious beast was lurking around the corner of her parents' house, she would've risked alerting her nosy sister and gone the other way. There was only a fifty-fifty chance that Haylee was waking her daughter from a nap right now and would spy Sadie's escape out her bedroom window. She'd gladly take those odds if she still had the choice.

With his eyes locked on Sadie, Ed reached his mouth up to a tree branch and took a leisurely bite. As if taking his time deciding what he was going to do about her.

Born and raised in Alaska, Sadie had encountered her share of moose. But the only time she'd ever been this close to one was at the Anchorage Zoo. And that one time a moose walked up to her bedroom window in her first-floor apartment and peered in. But there'd been no fear of being charged in either of those scenarios.

"The trees across the street taste better," she said to the animal, knowing it was impossible Ed understood her, but hoping for a miracle anyway. She needed to leave before Conner Michaelson arrived, and she preferred to do that in one piece rather than as a trampled pile of broken bones stuffed into an ambulance.

Family dinner was a weekly event. It was an unspoken rule that unless you had a very good reason not to be seated at the table at six p.m. sharp, you better be there. Sadie couldn't exactly tell her mom—or anyone else for that matter—that the reason she was skipping out was to dodge Conner. She'd never intended to crush on her oldest brother's best friend. Marc would *kill* her if he found out. It was easier to avoid Conner in such intimate settings and therefore not risk giving away her stupid feelings.

Plus, she was on a dating hiatus for the foreseeable future. Although, the dim-witted butterflies in her stomach that fluttered every time the unfairly, ridiculously attractive veterinarian entered her orbit apparently hadn't gotten the message.

"I'm just going to back up," she said to Ed. "I'm not bothering you, okay?"

At her first cautious step backward, the moose chomped a little slower, his ears flickering up and down once.

Sadie stilled, knowing better than to believe she wasn't in danger. One wrong move and Ed might lunge at her. Flatten her like a pancake with very little effort. She'd come too far these past ten months. Made too much progress. It'd be really inconvenient and crappy to be taken out now by the local celebrity moose. "Oh, the irony," she mumbled under her breath.

Sadie managed three agonizingly slow steps backward before Ed stopped eating, seemingly assessing the threat she posed to him. Silly moose. She was only a woman. A buck thirty-five—okay, thirty-*eight* because strawberry cheesecake ice cream was life—compared to his fourteen-hundred-pound frame. She posed exactly zero threats. Why didn't he get that?

"Hey, it's all good, Ed. I'll, uh, get you some blueberries, okay? You like blueberries." Locals were not supposed to feed the moose. She'd been told that only a hundred times growing up. She could practically hear Mrs. Nelson's voice in her head. *They could become dependent on human food sources and stop fending for themselves.* But loads of people in Sunset Ridge slipped Ed a treat a time or two. The moose was still plenty independent.

In fact, he never seemed to show up unless someone was about to fall in love. Or so the legend went.

"Do you know something I don't?" she whispered to Ed as she braved one more step backward. "Because I can't fall in love with Conner. You know Marc would *kill* me dead. Deader than dead." Even with the moose's attention fixated on her, she was more afraid of her older brother's wrath should he ever catch wind of her silly crush on his business partner. Never mind that she had less than zero intention of ever acting on it.

Of all the relationships she was working tirelessly to rebuild after being a crummy human being for most of her teenage years through her early twenties, Marc was the only one putting up one hundred and ten percent resistance. He was the oldest. The one who thought he knew everything about everyone. Had everyone figured out. He *knew* irresponsible, reckless Sadie was incapable of change. His mind was made up.

Luckily, Sadie's stubborn persistence could outlive them both.

She just had to overcome this stupid crush thing. *Then* she could prove to Marc that she had matured and turned a new leaf. Until she knew of a better way to stop her pulse from doubling every time Conner appeared, avoidance was her best option.

"I really need to go, *Ed*."

She waited, feet rooted in place, as Ed finished chomping on the snack between his lips. She was really regretting her footwear choice. Leave it to Sadie to pick the *cute* option instead of the practical one. If she tried to sneak back the way she came and was forced to run, she'd fall flat on her face for sure.

Her wedge sandals were not made for outrunning certain death.

When the last of the leaves disappeared from the moose's lips, he took two threatening steps forward. Sadie squeaked and flattened herself against the logs of the house. As he dug a hoof into the ground and snorted, she squeezed her eyes shut and braced for the worst.

This was it.

Death by the moose everyone in Sunset Ridge adored.

"Sadie?"

She slowly opened one eye, expecting to see the snout of a moose in her face. But Ed wasn't staring her down.

"Sadie, is that you?" a familiar voice called. A voice she really wished she hadn't memorized, even if it was completely accidental. It wasn't fair that Conner Michaelson not only looked like an Adonis, but sounded like one too. Now, her heart raced for an entirely different reason.

She opened the other eye and discovered the moose had vanished and the new local veterinarian was standing in his place. Darn the man and his friendly smile that could instantly turn any woman with a beating heart to goo. "Conner, hey."

"What are you doing?" he asked with too much curiosity. It would be so much easier if he treated her like she was invisible. But he was too kind for that. In the short three months he'd been in Sunset Ridge, he'd shown each and every member of the Evans family gratitude and interest. He knew everyone by name and remembered things people said at the dinner table from week to week.

Sadie wished she had that super power. It would come in handy during the remaking of herself into a better person. "There was a moose," she finally said as her senses came back to her, reminding her the beast could be nearby and ready to trample them both. If Ed injured the new vet everyone in Sunset Ridge adored, Marc would no doubt blame her for it.

She searched the surrounding area for the moose, but with the trees so thick around her parents' property, she couldn't see him. "You didn't see Ed, did you?"

"Ed." Conner chuckled. "No, I didn't. Wish I had, though. Seems like everyone has seen him *but* me. I hear he's a sort of urban legend around these parts."

"He's *something*, all right."

"You coming inside?" Conner asked, shoving his hands in the front pockets of his jeans. Sadie didn't mean to rake her gaze over his muscular body, but it happened anyway. He filled out a pair of jeans in a way that made her mouth water. Add that T-shirt whose sleeves were suffocating his biceps, and Sadie was in a whole lot of trouble. As if those dark brown eyes twinkling with kindness weren't dangerous enough.

This was exactly why she risked angering Mom by skipping out on dinner.

Stupid out-of-control-pulse.

"Yep. Coming inside. Don't have anywhere else to go."

Conner had been invited to every family dinner since he moved to town. Tonight was dinner number eleven. Not that Sadie was counting.

He was one of Marc's good friends from veterinarian school. He'd moved on a dime from Houston when Marc asked him to take the place of the retiring vet earlier that spring. Part of her wished Conner had shown up with a wife and six kids. Part of her was really glad he showed up single. The secret part of her that would never tell another soul. Not even Cody, the brother who'd always understood her better than the rest of her siblings.

"What's on the menu tonight?" Conner asked, completely unaware that she was desperate to avoid him. Oblivious to her pitiful crush. A crush she so did not want to have on the *one* guy Marc forbid her from getting involved with. Add to that threat that she wasn't healed from her last toxic relationship, and a crush was about the worst thing that could happen to her.

She'd made a resolution at the beginning of the year to stay single. For the *whole* year. A resolution she'd proudly announced to her entire family. Even if some of them had laughed, they *had* listened.

"Mom made oven-roasted chicken."

"Your family spoils me."

Oh, that smile. That bone-melting smile. She'd gladly give *both* her kidneys to know how well that smile could kiss.

Down, Sadie.

She had a lot of work to do before she let anyone get close again. She needed to prove to herself that when things went sideways, she could stand on her own two feet. Never again would she let a man destroy her from the inside out.

She didn't trust her own judgment anymore. She was always drawn to the smooth talker who looked all tempting and shiny on the outside but was a total nightmare on the inside. She'd been gaslighted enough with Aaron in their three-year on-again, off-again relationship to last her a lifetime. It left her wondering what a world without anxiety attacks even looked like.

Sadie stepped onto the porch and Conner held the door for her. Just in time for Marc to pull into the driveway and see them. *Just great.*

Conner waved at Marc and lingered on the porch. "I'll be right in."

Without an option to escape, Sadie reluctantly headed inside. It was just one dinner. She could make it through a single meal without acting like a pathetic teenager with a high school crush. She'd find a valid excuse to miss next week. And all the Sundays to follow until Conner no longer showed up like clockwork.

"What were you doing outside?" Haylee, her youngest sister, asked three steps from the front door. Sadie ignored the raised eyebrow and instead turned her attention to her one-year-old niece on her hip.

"Hey, Melly." Sadie tickled a soft finger beneath her chin until the little girl's blank, sleep-stricken expression gave way to a shy smile. "You want to come to your Aunt Sadie?" The adorable girl turned a bashful face into Haylee's shoulder. She definitely had Haylee's goofy expressions. But her eyes belonged to a father no one knew. No one except

Haylee. No amount of playing nice sister had earned Sadie that confidence.

"Nice try," Haylee said, unamused. "You were trying to leave, weren't you?"

"I was getting some fresh air." Okay, so lying kind of went against the whole *trying to be a better person* thing. But she couldn't breathe a word about her stupid, annoying crush and how out of hand it'd gotten lately. If Haylee slipped up and said something *near* Marc, he'd no doubt hear it with his bat-level ears.

"You're allergic to fresh air."

"Am not!"

"Every time I've asked you to come sit out by the fire pit with me, you've just laughed at me and plopped down in front of the TV instead."

"I don't like my hair smelling like smoke. Do you have any idea how many times I have to wash it to get the smell out—"

"Girls, can you set the table please?" Mom handed Sadie a pile of plates topped with silverware, cementing the fact Sadie wasn't getting out of this no matter what she did now. Dinner *did* smell delicious. Oven-roasted chicken with Mom's homemade mashed potatoes was her favorite. Which said a lot about her determination to leave tonight, especially when leftovers weren't guaranteed.

"I don't get you," Haylee said, following Sadie to the dining room.

Sadie focused on setting the plates in front of each of the chairs. Only six plus one high chair tonight. Unluckily for her, Cody and his wife Jenna were traveling along the West Coast for a week. She loved Jenna and was thrilled that a number of libraries had booked her to read her children's books during story hour. But without the one sibling who understood her best to save her from Marc, she felt the dread knot up in her stomach.

She counted the plates again. "Where's Laurel?" she asked of their oldest sister. "I need my Eli fix."

"Don't change the subject," Haylee said, maneuvering Melly into her high chair. The toddler was waking up, her eyes brightening with mischief. She was the cutest little girl on the entire planet. If Sadie never had kids on account of her indefinite single status, at least she would have a niece to spoil rotten. "You've been working so hard to prove to everyone that you're more responsible and reliable. Why would you flake tonight?"

It was no use pretending she wasn't trying to make an escape. The best she could hope for was to throw Haylee completely off the trail. "I had something I needed to take care of, that's all."

"Where?"

"What's with the nine hundred questions?" Sadie rolled her eyes playfully at Haylee. Their relationship was so much different than it had been a year ago. There was five years between them. They hadn't gotten along since Sadie entered high school. For a solid decade, they fought more than they did anything else. There'd been a lot of hair pulling and *Mom, she hit me! Mom, she stole my shirt!*

"I don't want you to screw this up," Haylee said, her voice low and honest.

"Screw what up?"

Before Haylee could answer, Marc and Conner's voices traveled down the hall and into the dining room. *Oh, Marc. Right.*

For months, Sadie had been trying anything and everything to prove to her oldest brother that she was turning a new leaf. She was Sadie 2.0. But it didn't matter what she tried—bringing him his favorite bacon, egg, and cheese bagel sandwich from MOOSE-CAKES by the clinic, making good on her promise to help him spring clean his massive yard—which had cost her an entire weekend and her favorite pair of jeans—or even showing up religiously for family dinners *every* Sunday for the past ten months. He was still convinced she'd never change.

"Will we be able to manage without her?" Conner asked Marc as they entered the dining room and took seats on the opposite side of the table. Sadie wished she didn't have to sit facing Conner. Especially since her brother had a front row seat to scrutinize every facial expression she made during dinner.

"It's only for a week," Marc said to Conner. "But you'd think Marylou thought we'd fed her to the wolves."

"I hope you two came hungry," Mom announced, carrying a covered casserole dish filled with the world's best oven-roasted chicken to the table. Dad followed behind with a giant bowl of mashed potatoes. Mom's homemade potatoes were almost better than strawberry cheesecake ice cream. Almost.

"I made extra," Mom said to Sadie.

"I don't understand how someone can love mashed potatoes so much," Haylee said with an eyeroll.

"It's because Mom measures the butter with her heart."

Conner let out a chuckle at her comment, warming her from the inside out. It drew her attention to his lips again, making her fingers itch with the need to comb through his beard. Until Marc's cold scowl landed on her. That straightened her out quicker than a cold shower. "My mom makes them the same way," Conner said, unaffected by Marc's grimace. "She sprinkles in some green onions too."

"Oh, I might have to try that next time."

"Mom, don't you dare contaminate my mashed potatoes," Sadie interjected. She looked at Conner and said, "Sorry. I can't stand onions."

"I guessed." Darn the man and his megawatt killer smile. That thing was dangerous when set loose. The only thing keeping her from overheating was Marc's icy glare. Some days Sadie felt certain Marc had convinced Conner to move to Sunset Ridge just to test her. Except, Conner *was* an exceptional vet. Every day she worked at her parents' store, she overheard praises for Dr. Michaelson.

Just as everyone was getting seated, Marc's phone vibrated obnoxiously loud against the table.

Mom lifted a scolding eyebrow at him.

"Sorry," he said, sending the call to voicemail. "Marylou is having a mild meltdown."

"Oh, no," Mom said as she handed the bowl of mashed potatoes to Conner. Wise decision to ensure Sadie got them last or there wouldn't be anything left to share. "I hope she's okay. Do I need to make a casserole?"

"No, Mom," Marc said. "Judy had to leave for Fairbanks tonight last minute. Her sister's in labor and all alone. Her husband's deployed and isn't due to be stateside until next week. She's going to help with the baby until he gets back."

"That was kind of her," Mom said.

His phone vibrated against the table again. Marc sent it to voicemail *again* and typed out a quick text. "Marylou is convinced the world will crumble and fall next week. We've been slammed at the clinic and she doesn't think she can cover the front desk alone with how busy we've been."

"Did you call around?" Dad asked.

"Called every clinic within fifty miles to see if they could spare someone, but no dice." Marc picked through the chicken, taking all the drumsticks. Sadie glared at him, but *that* he didn't seem to notice.

"I'll pop up front and help Marylou out when I can," Conner offered.

"It won't stop her from panicking," Marc said. "But it'll have to do. What other choice do we have? I wasn't about to ask Judy to stay behind and leave her sister to fend for herself. Baby came early and there might be complications."

An idea struck Sadie so suddenly it nearly knocked her off her seat. It bubbled up inside her, daring her to entertain it, despite its ludicrous nature. Marc would *never* go for it, even if Dad gave her some time off from the family store.

But Sadie didn't seem to have the good sense to keep it to herself. Not when she saw the golden opportunity to prove herself to Marc. "I could help out," she offered. "Marylou, I mean. I could help her out this week." She looked toward Dad at the head of the table. "If that's okay with you?"

"Things are slow right now," Dad agreed.

"I'll still come in to stock—"

"No." Marc's firm denial was expected.

"Why not?" Sadie shot back, holding her ground.

"You have no experience."

"It's answering phones, scheduling appointments, helping people fill out patient forms, that sort of thing, right?" It was a terrible idea when she considered how much time that would put her in close proximity to Conner. But if things were truly as busy as Marc suggested, she'd hardly see him anyway. "I was an executive assistant in Anchorage." Never mind that she was fired from that position for throwing herself at her boss at an office party. *Not* her proudest moment. But that was beside the point. The point was that she'd been good at her job.

"You should take the help," Dad insisted.

Sadie smiled her appreciation his way.

"This isn't some ticket to goof off," Marc said.

"I'm not *ten*."

"Are you sure about that?" he shot back. "Last I checked you've been fired three times I know about. Probably more."

Irritation simmered inside her, threatening to turn into an all-out boil. But Sadie hadn't spent ten months practicing yoga and meditation—never mind that she wasn't particularly good at either one—to lose her cool now. Especially when Marc seemed to be banking on it if the daring glimmer in his eyes was any indication. "I'll work for free."

Marc just laughed, something he infrequently wasted time doing. But Sadie didn't appreciate his rare smile aimed at her as a weapon of mockery. "I bet you don't last a day."

Sadie had her stubbornness to thank for being too proud to die of embarrassment in front of Conner. Too much was riding on her proving Marc wrong. Oh, she would *love* watching him eat his words. "What time do I show up tomorrow?"

"Seven thirty."

Ouch. That was early. Sadie mostly worked nights at the family store. She spent evenings on the register until close, then used the quiet time to restock shelves and work on her secret marketing campaign. Rumor had it Dad was trying to sell the store. But if she helped make it crazy profitable with her skills, maybe he'd reconsider. But that was another matter. *One hurdle at a time, Sadie.*

"Too early for you, princess?"

Oh, how she *hated* when he called her that. Treating her like she was still a kid rather than the twenty-six-year-old adult she was. "Nope." She almost told him she'd come in earlier, but the whole concept of under-promise, over-deliver had been drilled into her at her last job. She was keeping that ace up her sleeve. "I'll be there at seven thirty."

Chapter Two

CONNER

Belly stuffed and heart full, Conner Michaelson pulled into the driveway of his rental a little after eight. Boomer waited eagerly in the living room window both to greet him and to see what tasty leftovers Beth Evans sent along. The quirky pup who was, best to his knowledge, some mixture of German shepherd, husky, and a sprinkle of mystery, lifted one ear and left the other limp. The goofy image always made Conner smile, reminding him how lucky he was to have the dog in his life.

They'd found each other when they both needed someone most—after Mom remarried and stopped calling him to come fix things around the house; after his fiancée upended his life and left him more untrusting than he'd ever been. Driving home that dreadful day everything he thought he knew had been turned upside down, he discovered Boomer in the pouring rain cowering in a drainage ditch.

Every other car drove by without stopping, but Conner turned around at his first opportunity.

With nothing more than the suit he was wearing, a couple of dog biscuits in his glove box, and a slip leash he didn't end up needing, he coaxed Boomer to him. He wrapped him in his suit jacket and took him home. His car had been a muddy, soggy mess, but all these months later, he had zero regrets.

Cutting the engine, Conner checked his phone out of habit but was unsurprised that the only notification was an email advertising organic dental chews. Not even his sister needed him now that she was engaged to a man who knew exactly how to help her through her anxiety attacks.

"Boomer, buddy!" Conner knelt and embraced the eager pup with both arms the second he was through the door. He welcomed the licks to the cheek that made Boomer so happy he got crazy eyes. "Did you miss me?"

Beth insisted Boomer could attend Sunday

family dinner whenever Conner wanted to bring him, but the shepherd had some work to do when it came to table manners. It didn't help that Conner readily shared most anything he ate. As a vet, he knew better than to feed him Cheetos and kettle corn. But with the rough go he suspected Boomer had prior to that day they were united, Conner decided a few indulgences were only fair.

"Want to go outside and see if Miss Edith's ready?" he asked the pup as he pushed himself back up to standing.

Boomer bolted for the back door, his tail wagging fast enough to start a cyclone. He kept throwing glances over his shoulder that seemed to say *what's taking you so long, Dad?* He really was the best. Ten thousand Instagram followers thought the same thing. Only last week, one of them had mailed Boomer a travel water bowl. Conner grabbed it, a bottle of water, and a leash, and headed out back.

Focusing on the pup's eagerness helped distract him from the barren walls and sparce furniture. A reminder that though Conner found a place that needed him, he wasn't yet convinced things would work out. Wasn't ready to get too comfortable. He'd learned the hard way that complacency could have dire consequences. Though he had a good setup in

Sunset Ridge, it would take more than a couple months to stop expecting the other shoe to drop.

"How was dinner with the Evans clan?" Edith Banks asked from the other side of the fence as she stripped garden gloves and reached a hand to the back of Boomer's neck. He was propped on two paws on the three-foot fence between their yards so she could reach the spot behind his ears.

"Wonderfully filling, as always."

"And the company?"

"Small crowd tonight." Boomer, satisfied with his greeting, pushed off the fence and took off in zoomies around the backyard before getting down to business. "Sadie's going to fill in for Marylou for the week." He still wasn't sure how to feel about it, considering Marc's reaction. He'd been around the Evans family long enough to figure out the two siblings were at odds more than any others. But why Marc was so convinced Sadie would fail before she even tried nagged at him.

He'd been friends with Marc since vet school. Conner respected him as both a veterinarian and a friend. He trusted his judgment. Or always had, until he met Sadie Evans. He couldn't decide *why* he didn't agree with Marc, only that he didn't. A gut instinct. Something that hassled him in whispers he couldn't quite discern. But what did he know about reading people? If he was any good at it, Veronica would never have fooled him so easily. So effortlessly.

"You know, I've always liked Sadie," Edith mused, reaching for her light jacket draped in waiting over the back of a patio chair. Sunday evening walks were fast becoming a tradition during the summer season. "I might not be with the popular vote on that one, but I admire her persistence. When that girl puts her mind to something, she doesn't quit."

He remembered Marc's comment about her being fired three times, but he didn't want to stir up rumors. He and his neighbor had become fast friends, but that didn't mean he wanted to earn a reputation as a gossip by asking prying questions Edith may or may not even have the answers to. *Hmm. Maybe I want this to work out more than I realized.*

"Boomer, let's go."

The shepherd bolted from the opposite corner of the fenced-in backyard and nearly knocked Conner over in the process. After a very enthusiastic lick to the chin, Conner clipped the leash onto his collar.

The three set out on a route that had quickly

become routine three times a week. They meandered through the charming residential neighborhood and headed west toward the water where the sun hung high in the horizon. Conner was still getting used to the endless summer daylight. The sun setting at eleven.

"My husband and I used to go fishing at midnight," Edith offered, as if reading his mind. Or perhaps she caught him staring at the sun's unusually high position in awe.

"Midnight?"

"It's dusky then. But you can bait a hook without a flashlight." They waited as a lone car passed, then crossed the street, taking the sidewalk that followed the shore. A couple of joggers off in the distance wove through the sprinkles of wandering tourists. It amazed Conner how alive such a small, remote town could feel. "You should try it sometime," Edith added after several beats of silence.

"Midnight fishing?"

"Great way to woo a born-and-bred Alaskan girl."

Ah, this again.

He spread his lips in an amused smile. At least once a week, his widowed neighbor hinted Conner should find himself a wife through her unsolicited dating advice. She thought it was a shame that he, a man nearing thirty-three, should be single. Edith meant well—of that he was certain. But Conner was no longer sure he *wanted* a wife. It was only a miracle he dodged the bullet he had.

Conner had alluded to a relationship that hadn't worked out early in their friendship. But he hadn't offered up details. Hadn't wanted to relive that humiliation. How had he missed the signs? "Is that how George won you over?" he asked, hoping to divert. "Midnight fishing?"

"Oh, he got me hook, line, and sinker long before that," Edith admitted, a bashful glow stretched across her features. "But the midnight fishing helped seal the deal. Really, you should try it. Surely there's a woman who's at least caught your eye by now. You've certainly caused enough of a stir with the eligible women in this town."

"You make it sound like I'm on a dating show."

"Now, there's an idea."

He chuckled, convinced she was joking. But the seriousness in Edith's expression gave him pause. "They don't do that here, do they?" He was almost afraid to know the answer.

"Oh, no. We haven't been scoped out for reality TV yet."

He breathed a surprising sigh of relief.

"But there *is* a bachelor auction this year at the Blueberry Festival. It's next weekend. Not too late to throw your name in the hat."

Conner felt a little green. "No, thanks."

"It's for charity," she added. "All proceeds are going to the local animal shelter. They're in desperate need of renovations, as I'm sure you're aware."

Of that, Conner was. He, like Marc, volunteered a shift a week to administer checkups and immunizations. The facility was in less than ideal condition. But it was sanitary, stayed stocked with enough food to keep everyone fed, and better than no shelter at all. Still, Conner couldn't fathom offering himself up on a stage and going on a date with the highest bidder. He'd make an anonymous donation instead.

"What could it hurt?" Edith pressed when he didn't respond to her earlier spiel. "Unless you're saving yourself for someone special?" She stared at him as they walked, as if searching for the answer. "Is there someone you're sweet on already?'

"No, of course not. I'm still getting settled in. Focusing on one thing at a time."

That Sadie Evans was the first woman who popped into his head confused him. He admired her spunk and determination. But she was Marc's little sister. Considering the rift between the two siblings, he didn't think it'd be wise to pursue Sadie in any romantic way. Even if he found a way to trust his own judgment again when it came to women, he'd never allow himself to entertain those thoughts about Sadie.

"Any luck on finding a house yet?" she pressed, gently.

He was relieved for the subject change, but he'd have to keep an eye on Edith. She might sign him up for the auction and forget to tell him until the day of the festival. "Not yet." Conner's short-term lease on his rental would end in a couple of months. His landlord had made it clear that he wouldn't be able to extend as another family already applied for a year-long lease. But of the few houses for sale in Sunset Ridge, none felt like *home*.

"You're not sure about staying," Edith said matter-of-factly.

Or maybe *that's* why none of those houses felt like home. "My family's back in Houston," he admitted, feeling a pang of longing for the people who used to be so frequent in his life.

"It *is* hard," Edith agreed. "I left behind my family, too, when I met George." They approached a bench that was a regular pit stop on their route. Conner expanded the rubber collapsible bowl gifted to Boomer by one of his many fans and filled it with water. The pup could easily have gone the whole walk before even thinking about a drink, but he knew Edith needed the rest even if she'd never admit it.

Though Conner's family didn't seem to need him anymore, it was still an adjustment being half a world away. If something happened, it would take an entire day of flights to get back. He didn't feel reassured by that.

"Any regrets?" Conner asked as Edith sat on the bench and peered out at the bay. Conner pulled out his phone to snap a picture of Boomer enjoying his new present and quickly posted it with a tagged thank-you so Edith wouldn't scold him about living in the moment.

"No," Edith answered, softly stroking Boomer's neck as he slobbered his water all over the pavement. Her answer came so easily, but without much to explain why. Conner didn't press. Edith was an open book on most topics. But she no doubt had her secrets, just like he did. Secrets that may be best kept in the dark. "Come sit down. You're missing the sunset."

He obeyed readily and quickly forgot about the

past that kept him up most nights. The bay view with mountains stretched around it was almost enough to convince Conner Alaska was his new home. He'd never lived anywhere with such beauty. A landscape that could captivate a person so fiercely that it was easy to lose track of time. "I don't think I'd ever get tired of this," he admitted.

"I haven't, and it's going on forty-two years."

Boomer rested against his leg, positioning himself to get pets from both of them. Conner asked, "Do you think you'll stay in Sunset Ridge?"

"Now that George is gone and my kids and grandkids are scattered all over the country?"

"Yeah."

"I haven't decided. I can't imagine leaving my home. Leaving George's memory. But the winters are getting harder on these old bones." She stood, signaling she was ready to continue. Boomer hopped up on all fours, tail swishing eagerly as he waited for Conner's nod to continue their adventure.

"I'm not looking forward to all the cold and darkness." Conner shook out the rubber bowl and pressed it flat as they waited for a group of four to pass by. Boomer stayed by Conner's side obediently—they'd worked really hard at that one—but he stared the group down with his crazy, intense look that demanded friendship. The pup was rewarded with a few smiles, but no pets.

"Too much Texas in you." Edith chuckled. With a nudge of her elbow to his arm, she added, "That's why you should find yourself a wife. Someone to help keep you warm in the winter."

"One thing at a time," he reminded.

Edith returned a gentle smile that bordered on mischievous.

They strolled in companionable silence for the remainder of the walk, both enjoying the scenery and pleasantly warm summer air. It gave Conner ample time to gather his thoughts. To appreciate how lucky he was to have Marc's family in town who welcomed him with open arms as if he were one of their own. Beth ensured he stayed fed. Marc's brother-in-law, Chase, invited him to watch the baseball game Tuesday night. Here in Sunset Ridge, he felt part of something again.

If he wasn't so jaded on love, he might even entertain the idea of finding a wife and settling down, as Edith frequently suggested.

"Thank you for the walk, as always," Edith said when they returned home.

"Our pleasure."

She rubbed both hands on either side of

Boomer's face, and he snuck a lick to her wrist. They said their good-nights and went their separate ways.

Conner hardly had the deadbolt flipped on the front door when his phone rang. The call surprised him. It was not only late by Alaska standards, but later still in Houston. His worries that something might've happened back at home were quickly dismissed when an unprogrammed number appeared on his screen.

As the vet on call this weekend, he couldn't ignore it.

"Conner Michaelson?" The female voice on the other end sounded stiff and official. It gave him an uncomfortable chill.

"Speaking."

"I'm Detective Harlow."

Conner felt his legs weaken and sank onto his recliner. He thought all this was behind him now. "What can I do for you, Detective?" It was a fight to keep his voice even. He was shaky, both from fear and utter frustration. He'd done the right thing, even though it wasn't his mess to clean up. No charges had been filed.

Without so much as a clinical apology for the late hour, she dove right to the point. "I was wondering if you have any information about the whereabouts of your fiancée, Veronica Westin."

"She's not my fiancée anymore, Detective. Hasn't been in months." Conner welcomed Boomer as he shoved his head under Conner's hand and demanded pets. The pup knew Conner needed to keep his hand busy. "I haven't seen Veronica since we parted ways. I haven't kept in contact with her, either."

"Her call records indicate a number of text messages sent to you as recently as last week," Detective Harlow said.

"I last saw her the day after Christmas last year." The same day he forced her to come with him to the nonprofit's office she'd worked at for two years to admit what she'd done. To pray they'd accept his generous donation to make up for what she'd stolen and couldn't repay. He dropped her off at the airport and washed his hands of her as he drove away. "That's the same day I blocked her number. If she's been reaching out, I have no knowledge. I assure you, I have no interest in ever speaking to her again."

"You're absolutely sure she hasn't contacted you in any other way?"

"It has to be midnight where you're at," Conner

said, not as successful as he'd hoped in hiding his annoyance. "What is it you want, Detective?"

"Actually, I'm in Anchorage."

"Anchorage?"

"We have reason to believe your fiancée—"

"*Ex*-fiancée," Conner quickly corrected.

"—is in Alaska."

Conner rubbed his temple hard. He wasn't an investigator by any stretch of the imagination, but he'd watched enough crime dramas to sense something was off about all this. If they were looking for Veronica and suspected he was harboring her, he wouldn't be getting a phone call. He'd have an unannounced visitor hoping to catch her off guard. "I haven't seen her since December twenty-sixth, Detective."

"If you do, you'll call me at this number?"

"Sure." Before the call ended, Conner managed to slip in one last question. "What exactly has she done?"

"Nothing she hasn't done before. You should've turned her over to the authorities when you had the chance." With those ominous words, the call went dead.

Dread filled Conner's stomach, twisting it in knots he hadn't experienced since Veronica confessed to stealing twenty-five thousand from a children's charity. Which left him to wonder two things. How much had she stolen this time? And how much would it mess up the good thing he had going in Sunset Ridge when she no doubt tried to drag him down with her?

Chapter Three

SADIE

Sadie balanced two full drink carriers in both hands as she kicked the door of her sedan closed. She was half an hour early, despite the coffee run, and quite proud of herself for it. She couldn't wait to see the look on Marc's face when he realized she beat *him* to the clinic. He'd underestimated her, as always.

"Need a hand?"

Her heart went all aflutter at the soothing sound of Conner's voice, warning her she'd have to be on her best behavior if she wanted this to work. With any luck, Conner would be so busy with patients she'd hardly see him. "I've got it, thanks," she said over her shoulder, sensing his approach from behind.

"Coffee smells wonderful," he said with a slight yawn as he came into her sightline. Lines tugged at the corners of his eyes that suggested sleep the night before was scarce. "We have a coffeemaker in the break room, but I think it's older than Marc."

"Let me guess," Sadie said. "He refuses to replace it even though it's on its last leg?"

Conner's easy smile turned her insides to melty goo. Even tired, the man was a swoon-hazard. "You nailed it."

She forced herself to look away as he unlocked the clinic door, determined to focus on the mission. If it killed her, she'd prove to Marc that not only was she no longer unreliable and immature, but she'd picked up some valuable skills at her last job that might even impress him if only he gave her the chance.

As Conner flipped on the lights, Sadie set the drink carriers on the front counter. Other than her brother, who drank his coffee blacker than the Alaska night sky in the darkest days of winter, she wasn't certain what anyone else preferred. She'd ordered a variety of Black Bear Coffee's most popular drinks and hoped for the best.

"What's your poison?" Sadie asked Conner. "I have a caramel macchiato, a white chocolate mocha, an Americano—"

"I'll take whatever's left," Conner answered as he stepped next to her, whooshing a cloud of intoxicating cologne as he arrived. He slipped her a glance that temporarily made her forget where she was and what she was doing. She wasn't foolish enough to think Conner reciprocated secret feelings for her. He was way out of her league. His kindness came only because he was Marc's closest friend. This crush of hers was definitely one-sided. "Let everyone else choose one first."

Focus, Sadie. She twisted the coffees one by one, turning the cups decorated with blue forget-me-nots to better showcase the handwritten flavors. "Do you know when Marylou—"

"You haven't been here five minutes and already you're harassing Conner."

Marc's unexpected voice startled Sadie, causing her hand to slip. The caramel macchiato fell against her chest, spilling a few drops onto her white silk blouse. But before she could get a solid grip on the cup, it slipped from her fingers and crashed against the tile floor. Coffee exploded in all directions, covering the floor, splashing the counter front, drenching the bottoms of her light-gray dress pants, and soaking the soles of her bright-red heels. It was only because she served as a human shield that Conner seemed spared of the disaster.

"We have a coffeemaker," Marc said, his tone chilling enough to stop the glaciers from melting for another century.

"Let me grab some paper towels," Conner said, his soft tone extending kindness.

"Let Sadie," Marc insisted. "Maybe the cleanup will be a reminder that this isn't some corporate office environment."

Conner didn't listen, thankfully.

It took every ounce of restraint Sadie had, and several she didn't, not to spin on her brother and give him a piece of her mind. Because she knew that's what he expected. What he was no doubt counting on so he had a reason to show her the door on day one. "I have a black coffee for you," she said to Marc with a forced smile as she accepted a handful of paper towels from Conner and began mopping up the counter.

"Already told you, we have a coffeemaker."

She waited for him to disappear into the back, but he stood at the door watching instead. A hint of amusement played at the corner of his mouth. Not enough to qualify as a smile, or even a smirk. Marc seemed to be allergic to those. "You going to stare or help?" Sadie fired, unable to help herself.

"Conner, we need to go over the patient list," Marc said, ignoring Sadie's question. Something he'd later call an outburst. She loved her oldest brother, but sometimes he could be a huge thorn in her side. He was grumpy by nature, except when it came to the animals. But his attitude this morning was pushing the limit.

"I'll be right there." Conner stood, holding a pile of coffee-drenched towels.

"I can take those," Sadie offered. When he seemed to hesitate, she added, "You have more important things to attend to, Dr. Michaelson." She didn't *mean* to flirt, but she'd never called him that before, and it came out more playful than she intended. "Thank you for your help."

He nodded and followed Marc into the back.

Sadie kicked off her wet heels and fished a mop out of the janitor's closet to finish cleaning the sticky floor, ignoring the damp fabric of her dress pants clinging to her ankles. No way was she running home to change. She'd spend most of her time behind the counter, out of sight, anyway.

She slipped her phone from her pocket and shot

a quick text to Haylee requesting a wardrobe change. But with how many times she'd heard her sister get up last night with Melly, she suspected that SOS would go unanswered for hours yet.

"Already on your phone," a woman mumbled, drawing Sadie's attention to the front door. Marylou Carlson, a woman a few years older than Sadie's mom, took her time getting to the front counter. Even without her high heels, Sadie towered at least four inches over the woman. But what intimidation her height couldn't offer, her icy, suspicious glare made up for.

"I was just texting my sister—"

"Look, I appreciate you helping out. I do," Marylou said, subtly nudging Sadie out of her way to get to her chair. "But if you're going to spend all your time on your phone, you might as well go home now."

Sadie shouldn't be surprised that Marc had spoken to Marylou ahead of time about this arrangement. She took a deep, centering breath. Something that had become second nature to her in these past few months. "I'm here to work," Sadie said firmly. "Tell me what you need me—"

"Why are there drops of coffee on my files?"

"There was a casualty—"

"Get those away from the front desk," Marylou said, pointing at the drink carriers.

"Did you want—"

"Either put them in the break room or toss 'em." Marylou dropped into her rolling chair and powered on her computer. "No open beverages allowed up here. Got it?" Sadie nearly argued that the coffees had stoppers, but she bit her tongue. It was doubtful Marylou would care. She didn't need to make an enemy on day one. That was the *old* Sadie. "And put your shoes on. We're not running a barn."

Two vet techs arrived as Sadie slipped her feet into soggy shoes.

"Is that coffee?" one girl asked with wide, appreciative eyes. She, along with the other tech, seemed younger than Sadie, but that didn't stop an unwarranted pang of jealousy, knowing Conner worked closely with both these gorgeous women all day long.

"Sure is," Sadie said, following them into the back and rattling off the different orders. Hoping to make a couple of allies. She could certainly use them.

"Please tell me the mocha has an extra shot," the other girl said as Sadie set the drink carriers on the lone breakroom table. One Sadie recognized from years ago. The well-worn table used to take up residence in the family room, but when Mom announced she wanted to throw it out, Marc kept it.

"They all do," Sadie answered, her optimism from earlier this morning returning. "It's Monday, after all."

"You're a life saver!"

Before Sadie could introduce herself, Marc stormed into the room and headed right for his ancient coffeemaker. It made noises that didn't seem to comply with the fire code. "I have a black coffee for you," she tried once more.

"Why aren't you up front? Phones turn on in five minutes."

Sadie instantly thought of half a dozen retorts, but managed to swallow them all. *You're better than this, remember?* She knew better than to expect to win her brother over in a single morning. With a forced smile, she left the coffees behind, mourning the loss. Without the nectar of the gods to pull her through this already long morning, the day promised to try every last nerve.

She caught a glimpse of Conner at the opposite end, looking dashing as ever—if not a bit worn out— as he slipped into his white lab coat. He seemed the most easygoing guy she'd ever met. What could possibly be troubling him? She was so consumed with her thoughts that the door to the lobby nearly smacked her. An inch closer and she'd have a bruise in the center of her forehead.

"Are you coming or not?" Marylou demanded.

The morning flew by in a blur of patients, an endlessly ringing phone, and all-around chaos. Haylee sent an apology text at eleven rather than bringing a change of clothes, but Sadie decided it was for the best. She'd chased not one, not two, but *three* escape artists in her still damp-soled high heels. The third capture resulted in a broken heel and a fully slobbered blouse. Probably because it tasted of peppermint mocha.

She was covered head-to-toe in dog hair of all varieties and breeds. Probably cat hair too, though the three feline patients had arrived in carriers and yowled their disdain every second they were in the clinic.

"I'm going on lunch," Marylou announced, pushing up from her chair. "Think you can keep the place from burning down?" Though her tone wasn't nearly as harsh as it'd been first thing this morning, Marylou was far from warming to Sadie. At least she trusted her enough to leave the building.

"I've got it covered."

"Phones are switched off through the lunch hour, but doors stay open. There won't be any patients until one." Marylou shouldered her purse. "If anyone shows up early—"

"I'll have them fill out the forms if they're not already entered in the computer."

Marylou nodded, which was nearly as good as a smile. "You can grab a break when I get back." With that, she marched toward the front door as if being chased. Seemed Marylou couldn't get away from Sadie fast enough. Not that she could blame her. Sadie was a quick learner, but she asked a million questions along the way. Questions that individually drove Marylou to groaning and terse smiles. The cacophony of them had her muttering about taking up smoking again after twenty years.

When the door closed, Sadie let out a heavy sigh of relief for the first time since she arrived at the clinic this morning. There was still plenty of time for things to go wrong, and for Marc to witness them all. But she'd survived half the day. That was an accomplishment all its own.

Kicking off her soggy heels, she fished a protein bar and a bottle of water from her tote bag. As she twisted off the cap, Conner appeared in the lobby with Delilah Matthews and her caramel Yorkie tucked under her arm. "Thank you so much, Dr. Michaelson," the woman old enough to be Sadie's grandma cooed. "I'm so glad you're here. Waffles is lucky to have you. I don't know what I'd do if I lost him."

Conner patted her shoulder gently. "Just go easy on the cucumbers," he said while flashing his megawatt smile. He ran a finger under the Yorkie's chin, earning him some eager tail wags. "Too many at once is too much for his little tummy to handle."

Sadie's heart melted instantly. It wasn't enough that Conner was too attractive to be legal or one of the most kindhearted people she'd ever met. He had to be so *good* with animals too. No wonder half a dozen women brought in their pets this morning for *routine* checkups. Never mind that they weren't due for months.

As Delilah left, Sadie pretended to busy herself with coffee-splattered files.

"Tell me you're eating more than a protein bar for lunch?" Conner said, his honey smooth voice causing her pulse to double for the second time in three minutes. With the rush, Sadie hadn't seen him in a couple of hours. She wasn't thrilled about how much she missed him, or the torture she felt being teased that he was so close but out of reach. What a mess.

"I'll grab something when Marylou gets back," she lied. She desperately craved a break from the chaos, not that she'd ever admit it. But lunch wasn't even on her radar. She yearned for a drive to her favorite scenic pull-off a couple miles from town. It'd likely be crawling with tourists, but Sadie could ignore them easily enough. She just needed a few minutes to catch her breath, away from all distractions. To practice those meditation exercises she was so horrible at. Without a breather, she might not survive the day. And she wasn't about to let her brother have the satisfaction of her quitting on him.

"I have some leftover spaghetti," Conner said. "You're welcome to it."

Sadie immediately conjured an image of her white blouse covered in marinara. "Thanks, but I'll pass. I've tempted fate enough for one day." She held up the folder splattered most heavily in caramel macchiato as evidence.

"Someone should've warned you about Marylou's no-open-containers policy," he said, apology in his tone.

"And take all the fun out of it?"

"It wasn't fair," Conner said, his tone gentle yet

serious. It made Sadie feel . . . seen. Which would've been welcome aside from their complicated situation. Even worse was that Conner's simple statement made her feel vulnerable. She'd worked really hard never to feel that way again after her toxic disaster of a relationship.

"I know for tomorrow." She offered him a *don't worry about me* smile. "You doing okay?"

"Me?" He seemed taken aback by her question.

"You look a little . . . tired."

Conner pushed off the counter he'd been leaning against and rubbed his hand over the back of his neck. "Still adjusting to all this late-night daylight."

Sadie recognized his answer for what it was: avoidance. She went along with it because she was well acquainted with the tactic *and* the reason for using it. "You need blackout curtains." She carefully twisted the cap off her water bottle and took a sip.

"I suppose I do."

Sadie's phone vibrated against the counter, instantly drawing her attention. She figured it was Haylee offering to bring that change of clothes she no longer needed or Mom asking her to pick up some groceries on her way home. But the number tied with the text message wasn't one she recognized. Out of habit, she pulled the phone closer to read it.

Her stomach plummeted into her toes.

"Everything okay?" Conner asked, halfway to the door.

Sadie couldn't manage words, so she forced a nod instead. She couldn't tear her eyes from the screen, feeling sick. She'd blocked his number. And the two subsequent numbers he got after that. She'd also changed her own. Aaron shouldn't be able to bother her anymore. Her heart rate doubled, then tripled. Her entire body buzzed in chaos, warning her an anxiety attack was imminent unless she did something to immediately diffuse the bomb about to go off inside her.

"Sadie," Conner said, his tone soft and firm. He leaned over the counter, dropping a hand to her shoulder. Staring at her until she lifted her gaze to his. "Breathe."

His simple words offered reassurance she didn't deserve. She had no one to blame over the Aaron situation but herself. How many times had her friends and family told her to leave him? If only she'd listened early on. Or better yet, never met him at all.

"Take a deep breath in through your nose."

When she finally obeyed, it made her acutely aware of his warm hand pressed against her shoulder. Tingles of an entirely different variety danced up and down her arm. The warmth both soothed and distracted her. The early panic dissipated, as if it were never there at all. All that existed was this moment.

The bells above the front door clamored, announcing Marylou's return.

Conner straightened instantly, taking his delightfully warm hand with him. She felt the absence of his touch, making her painfully aware of one troubling fact. She was in way deeper than she thought.

With a couple more deep breaths, Sadie cleared her head enough to stuff her phone in her tote bag before Marylou found it out.

"Everything okay?" Marylou's question was laced in suspicion.

"Yep. It was quiet while you were gone." She yearned to run her phone over or throw it in the ocean. She hated how powerless a stupid text message could make her feel. Hated that Conner could so easily prevent an anxiety attack that had the promise of being a big one. Her life hadn't been fair in forever, and she was growing tired of that.

"Dr. Michaelson?"

"Everything was quiet, Marylou. Just as Sadie said."

"Can I take my lunch now?" Sadie asked,

avoiding Conner's concerned gaze. She only hoped he didn't mention anything to Marylou. Or worse, Marc.

"Sure, go ahead. But be back in an hour."

Sadie felt Conner's gaze follow her to the front door, but he thankfully didn't follow. She had enough to sort out without the too-attractive-for-his-own-good man clouding her senses. Her shoulder still tingled from where his hand had rested.

Desperate for fresh air, Sadie turned off her phone and headed for her favorite scenic pull-off to practice the meditation she was so terrible at. It was that or admit she was more than crushing on Conner Michaelson. She was full-on falling.

Chapter Four

CONNER

Conner collapsed in his recliner seconds after he made it inside. Boomer, thankfully, allowed their greeting to take place in Conner's lap. Never mind that the dog was eighty-five pounds and barely fit within the confines of the chair. He jumped at any chance to embrace his inner lap dog.

"Am I glad to be home," he said to the pup, who answered with a full-cheek lick.

After Sadie left for her lunch break, all chaos broke out at the clinic. If it wasn't enough that their schedule was packed, three emergencies came through the door. He and Marc divided and conquered to attend to it all. Marylou rescheduled the patients she could to accommodate the golden retriever who'd swallowed a phone charger, the tabby cat who'd ingested an entire lily, and the Persian who'd been having seizures.

They'd saved them all.

It felt great to be a part of something. *Really* a part of something. Sunset Ridge was certainly tugging on his heartstrings. He wondered if Marc realized how special his clinic was from others.

Which only made his stomach knot.

He hadn't heard from Detective Harlow today, but that didn't mean she wouldn't show up in town unannounced if she'd been in Anchorage last night. He only hoped that when she did, it wouldn't cost him everything he'd found here. This place was special. More than he ever thought it could be.

Or maybe he was drawn for another reason.

A fiery, redheaded reason who, despite every curveball thrown her way today, had pressed on. She'd shown up to the clinic in bright-red high heels and long, wavy hair styled to perfection. She looked ready to attend an executive board meeting. But by the end of the day, her nice clothes were ruined, her hair ended up in a messy bun, and she was walking with a forced limp because of a broken heel and Marylou's stubbornness about shoes.

And she did it all with a smile.

He'd never met a more determined woman in his life. It was a refreshing, and if he was being entirely honest, attractive quality.

Conner groaned away the thoughts of Sadie that shouldn't be lingering. Boomer, sensing his distress, gave him a big, sloppy chin-to-forehead lick. Or maybe the pup was eager to get out and stretch his legs.

"How many times did Miss Edith stop by and spoil you rotten today?" He rubbed Boomer good and thoroughly along both shoulders, making the dog moan in delight. His neighbor was a godsend who checked on Boomer regularly throughout the day when he worked. "Two or three times, huh, buddy?"

Boomer arched into the intense pets, subsequently smashing his chest against Conner's face, suffocating him a mouthful of dog hair.

Before Conner could contemplate how he was going to escape this eighty-five-pound trap, his phone buzzed in his shirt pocket. Boomer let out a bark, hopped off the recliner, and barked again. Dread instantly filled Conner, erasing the amusement of

Boomer's reaction. "So much for being left alone by the detective tonight," he murmured.

But it wasn't a random number on the screen.

"You're up late," he said to his sister.

"Hello to you, too," Katy teased.

"Everything okay?"

"Yes, big brother. Everything is fine." He could practically hear her eyeroll. Katy liked to pretend she had everything under control. Always had. But until she'd gotten engaged, she'd always been honest with him. Open. Vulnerable. He was truly happy she'd found someone. Someone good. Someone who wouldn't betray her or hurt her. But he missed being the one she turned to. He missed being needed.

"How's the wedding planning going?" he asked after a massive yawn that earned him a curious head tilt from Boomer. The pup was apparently worried their nightly walk was in jeopardy.

"That's why I'm calling, actually."

"Yeah?" He sat up straighter.

"Are you bringing a plus-one?"

"Katy, your wedding is six months away."

"I'm working on the seating chart." Her tone was much too nonchalant, tipping Conner off immediately.

"I'm not dating anyone if that's what you're

really asking." He'd been in Sunset Ridge just shy of three months. The whole debacle with Veronica had gone down two seasons prior. She couldn't seriously think he'd moved on already. Or that he ever would. "What are you worried about, Katy?"

"Nothing."

"Katy."

"I just want you to be happy," she finally admitted.

"I *am* happy. Today I saved a golden retriever who swallowed a phone charger. *And* put an elderly woman's worried mind at ease when I was able to diagnose her Yorkie's tummy troubles as a cucumber overdose."

"You know what I mean. Happy *with* someone."

He sat forward, dropping his elbows onto his knees. He was too tired for this discussion. Katy meant well. All the women in his life did, even if they were driving him a little crazy right now. The last thing on his mind was getting involved with a woman. Especially since Veronica's past seemed so set on haunting him.

Not that he would drag his family into *that* mess. He hadn't had the heart to call the authorities on his ex the day after Christmas. Now he was wondering if he made a mistake in handling things the way he had. Whatever Detective Harlow was digging up would be his problem to deal with, and his alone. "I'm still getting settled," he said, hoping the same answer he gave Edith would appease Katy.

"I heard there's a bachelor auction this weekend. Some festival or something."

He had no clue how she'd figured that out, unless Katy and Edith had somehow become secret long-distance friends. *Oh, the Internet.* "Not doing it."

"It's for charity, Conner. An animal shelter. Kind of up your alley. It would be a great way to fit into your new community, you know?"

Conner popped to his feet and Boomer let out a deep bowing stretch, hopeful their evening run was about to commence. The pup yearned to stretch his legs, and now so did Conner. He could only take so much in one day. "I'm fitting in just fine. Weren't you listening—"

"The sign-up form's online and super easy—"

"No." He rarely used such a stern tone, but when he did, Katy knew it meant he was serious. "Focus on planning your wedding. On *your* big day. Mine will come. Eventually." Or maybe not at all. Conner wasn't really trusting of women these days. Not with the way Veronica had so easily fooled him. Though the image of Sadie Evans covered in dog hair and coffee splatters did tug a gentle smile across his lips. But it was hardly enough to warrant thoughts about dating or marriage.

"Will you at least *think* about it?" Katy's quiet, slightly stung tone always got him.

"Fine."

"Yay!"

"I'll *think* about it. But if anyone's signing me up, it's me. Got it?"

"Yep, of course."

At long last, she let him off the hook where his mess of a love life was concerned and rambled on about wedding preparations. How she was going dress shopping with her bridesmaids and Mom next week, the elegant Christmas theme she was after, and a number of other details he had trouble focusing on. Conner listened as well as his tired brain could. What mattered most to him was her happiness. It radiated in her tone, and that brought him peace.

When she finally let him go, he forced himself to change into a pair of shorts and jogging shoes. On evenings the duo didn't walk with Edith, they ran. It wasn't Conner's favorite pastime, but Boomer loved it. And it did help distract him when he needed it. Tonight, he needed it. Big time.

They followed the same route as always, adding in an extra mile when they reached the bay walk. They stopped at the end of the pier, mostly so Conner could snap an Instagram-worthy photo of Boomer. The pup's followers would worry if they went more than twenty-four hours without an update. They begged for reels. Video clips instead of only still photos. But he wasn't techy enough for all that. Photos would just have to do.

He watched the sun disappear below the horizon as Boomer took in all the fresh smells drifting off the darkening water, bringing to light how long his sister had talked his ear off. "Better head back, huh?"

Boomer wagged his tail in earnest. The pup could outrun Conner tenfold if given the chance.

A gaggle of laughing tourists on the bay walk ahead caused Conner to pause. They seemed young and rowdy. No doubt they had a few drinks in them. At his threshold for the day, he wasn't in the mood to deal with them should they want to pet Boomer. Which was almost always the case in these situations, especially if they recognized him from social media.

Conner decided on a detour. Boomer didn't seem to mind the switch to the routine. He spent an inordinate amount of time sniffing the new air, happy to walk rather than run.

It wasn't until Conner spotted a mop of red hair that he realized they were walking by Evans' Outfitters, the Evans family's sporting goods store. But why Sadie was sitting on a bench at the back of it so late confused him. He remembered how tense she'd gotten when her phone buzzed earlier. He'd bet his next paycheck she'd been on the verge of an anxiety attack. Though grateful he'd been able to help, the whole scenario bugged him all day.

"Sadie?" he called out.

She sat up straight, seemingly startled. Quickly, she swiped under her eyes. He heard the unmistakable sound of sniffling. "Conner, hey."

"Everything okay?"

"Yeah." Boomer trotted to her, dropping his head in her lap and staring up at her, hopeful for attention. Sadie obliged right away, and he swore his heart softened. Veronica didn't mind dogs, as long as she could pet them on her terms. But Sadie allowed Boomer to call the shots and took every ounce of love he offered. *What a difference.* He shook away the unsolicited comparison. Sadie was a friend. Practically family.

"What are you doing out here?"

"I was working."

Conner glanced up toward the two-story warehouse-style building. "I didn't think the store was open this late."

"It's not." She dropped a kiss to Boomer's head, and he instantly hopped onto the bench and climbed into her lap. Or attempted to. When he realized his massive body wouldn't fit, he settled for half. Sadie wrapped her arms around him. Boomer was the best snuggler. "I do some of the stocking and stuff after hours."

"Aren't you tired?"

"Aren't you?"

"Touché."

Conner shifted his weight from one leg to another. Even if he wanted to sit down, Boomer had monopolized the bench. "Sadie, is everything really okay? I know you're pretty tough and resilient, but everyone has hard days."

She looked up at him, surprise in her eyes. "You think I'm resilient?"

"Of course, I do. You proved that today."

"You'd be the first to think so," she mumbled.

"Marc appreciates you more than he's willing to admit." Even if his friend hadn't spoken the words, one silent glance said it all. Marc knew as well as everyone else in the clinic that without Sadie there today, things could so easily have gone sideways. She went above and beyond. But why her brother couldn't *tell* her that frustrated Conner. Words of appreciation could go a long way toward mending whatever rift existed between them. *Not your place, Conner.*

"Marc's convinced I'm just going to flake tomorrow."

"Are you?"

"Of course not."

Conner took a seat on the sidewalk, proving he wasn't in a hurry. Hoping that if he settled in, Sadie might open up about that text message. It was likely a terrible idea, but he hated the thought of leaving her alone when she seemed to need someone. Even if her cheeks were dry, the glow of the streetlight hinted at their redness. "What's really going on?"

"You mean besides my brother being a giant pain in the—" She stopped herself before she finished her thought, but it didn't keep Conner from chuckling. After a seriously deep breath, she added, "I'm working on being a better person. So, I'll keep my thoughts to myself. But you get the gist."

Though he wanted to know more about what had created such a wedge between the siblings so he could decide whether he had any power to help mend it, it wasn't what he was really asking. "Who texted you today? While Marylou was on lunch."

He didn't miss how she hugged Boomer tighter. God love the pup who didn't squirm as he tilted his head up and caught her chin with a lick. "It doesn't matter," Sadie answered in a whisper so quiet he nearly missed it.

"Are you in some kind of trouble?"

"No." She shook her head into Boomer's neck. "I don't think so."

Her response caused him to bristle. A protective reflex he only ever felt about those he cared for most. When had Sadie gone from acquaintance to . . . *more*? Had it happened today at the clinic when she scraped a knee capturing a runaway border collie and handed him over to the tech with a smile? Or when she offered to help man the front desk without a second thought during family dinner? Or perhaps it'd been happening for weeks and he'd been unaware until this very crucial moment. A moment that made him realize he would go to extreme lengths to keep her safe. "If someone's bothering you, I'll take care of it."

Sadie lifted her chin from Boomer's fur and stared at him, genuine confusion lingering in her gaze. "Why would you do that?"

Her simple question answered so many of his. She had one of the most amazing families he'd ever met. A family who'd do anything to protect one another. Yet, she didn't seem to think that benefit extended to her. From anyone. His heart squeezed painfully. "I care about you, Sadie." The words were dangerous to speak aloud, but they were true. Words she *needed* to hear.

"You shouldn't waste your time. Haven't you heard? I'm an unreliable trainwreck." Before he could tell her she was wrong, she added, "And it's not just Marc who thinks that. I have a . . . track record. Ask anyone in my family."

"Sadie, who sent you the text?"

"Just an ex," she said dismissively. "It's nothing."

He didn't buy her answer for a minute. "You have one of those, too?" Though she said nothing, he did seem to have a captive audience and continued. "I was engaged, actually. Supposed to get married this summer."

"I had no idea."

"I never talk about it," Conner said with a mere shrug. His feelings about the whole situation were dulled from the time he'd had to reflect on all the red flags he missed. He dared to shift on the sidewalk, resting his back against the bench. Not quite touching Sadie's leg, but not as far away as he could be. He reached up to scratch Boomer behind the ears. "She lied to me about something pretty big. I don't know if I've ever felt more humiliated in my life. Not because she lied, but because I didn't see it coming."

"Then you *really* don't want to get any closer to me," Sadie said with a pitiful laugh.

"Why?"

"I can't count the number of lies I told my family over the two and a half years I was with Aaron." The admission that fell so easily from her lips seemed to startle her, and she buried her face in Boomer's neck. Her cheek brushed his fingers.

Conner inwardly gasped at the contact, surprised at the tingles of electricity that skittered up his arm. They pulled away at the same time. "You were covering for him?" he guessed, pretending the moment between them hadn't happened. Hoping to keep things neutral for more reasons than he could count.

"Yeah." The single word was laced with such sadness. It made Conner's chest ache.

"Did he ever hurt you?" he asked carefully.

"Did he ever hit me, you mean?" She shook her head, wiping away a tear with the sleeve of her sweatshirt. "Sometimes I think that would've been better than all the mind games. At least if he'd slugged me once, I would've left before things got so bad."

Conner lifted onto the bench, forcing Boomer to make room. He draped an arm around her, pulling her into him as she clung to the pup. Her lavender shampoo invaded his senses as she let out a few sobs, her tears soaking through his shirt. So many emotions warred inside him, but he pushed them all aside to focus on what mattered most in this moment. "Does Marc know?"

Sadie sat up and pulled out of his embrace. "No. And you can't tell him, Conner."

"Sadie—"

"I mean it. This is *my* mess." She kissed Boomer atop the head and shimmied out from beneath his bulky frame without displacing him, like some sort of ninja. "I have to finish up a few things in the store. Promise me you won't say anything. Not to Marc. Not to anyone."

"I won't, but—"

"Promise me." Arms folded across her chest, she stared at him hard. That determination was hardened in her eyes.

"I promise."

"Forget we talked about this, okay?"

"Sadie?"

"Hmm?" He could feel her antsy discomfort rolling off her in waves.

"No matter what you think, you didn't deserve any of it."

Sadie stared at him a few beats more, as if she might say something, but ultimately didn't. She left him on the bench as the shepherd combat-crawled into his lap and let out a whine.

His heart raced as the emotions he'd shoved down began to stir. The most prominent one shouldn't exist at all. He wasn't supposed to care about her like this. Not this deeply. He knew what it meant. Boomer whined again. "Are we both in trouble, buddy, or is that just me?"

Chapter Five

SADIE

Sadie sipped her strawberry margarita as she watched funny dog videos and waited for her sisters to arrive. Done were the days when she was always late or constantly cancelling. Done were the days that a trip home could be derailed last minute because Aaron didn't want her to leave and threatened to break up with her if she left rather than offer to come along like she'd asked him a thousand times. She got a chill thinking about him, wondering where the unsolicited thought had come from.

Oh, right. The stupid text message from yesterday. *I'll always find you, Love Bug. Always.*

She should've deleted it. The thought of it living on her phone made her squirm uncomfortably. She'd blocked the number minutes after the text appeared, but keeping it was a reminder that she could never *ever* let her guard down.

Out of habit, she scanned the tables and bar area inside Warren's Sea Shack. Only after she checked—twice—did she let out the breath she'd been holding.

Safe.

She returned her attention to her phone and the golden doodle walking on his two hind legs, helping himself to a pizza on the kitchen counter. Unaware he was already caught. If only one could get paid to watch dog videos. She'd be an easy millionaire by now.

When her phone pinged, she jerked in her high-top stool. After determining it wasn't an unsolicited message from her past, she returned to breathing normally for the two point three seconds it took her brain to register the text sender. *Conner.*

Conner: Be honest. Is this photo Instagram worthy?

Sadie drew her eyebrows together, seriously concerned that Conner was a little more into himself than he let on. He could break the social media platform with his swoonworthy smile alone, but that didn't mean he should try. But in the middle of firing a response that questioned if he was *that* kind of guy, a photo of Boomer wearing a Chicago Cubs bandana around his neck appeared in her feed.

The pup looked ridiculously happy with one ear standing tall and the other at half-mast. Last night when Conner had found her on the bench outside the family store, she wished she could take Boomer home for the night. Or kidnap him indefinitely. If it killed her, she was going to find a place to rent in town that allowed her to have a big, huggable dog.

Sadie: He looks dashing!
Sadie: But there's no way Marc will let Boomer in the door wearing that.
Sadie: Does he know you're a Cubs fan?

Familiar giddy feelings coursed throughout her body as she awaited his response. Until this morning, they'd never exchanged numbers. But Conner insisted he put his number in her phone *just in case*. He hadn't had a chance to elaborate on the meaning of that because Marc burst through the door seconds later like a bad storm.

It didn't *mean* anything. Conner was just looking out for her. He was a friend of the family who'd proven time and time again that he took an interest in everyone. He offered help whenever the opportunity arose, whether it was washing dishes or building a woodshed. He would keep her secret, as she asked. But he wouldn't leave her high and dry should an actual conflict arise because of it. The sentiment made her feel warm and squishy inside. She ignored that whispered warning that did its best to convince her it was all too good to be true.

Conner: He'll get over it.
Sadie: Ten bucks says Marc has something to say about the bandana before you even get the front door closed behind you.
Conner: A bet?
Sadie: I don't recommend it, because I'll definitely win.
Conner: You're on!

Sadie sipped her margarita to hide the enormous smile she had no right wearing. This conversation, however friendly, shouldn't be happening between them. Any progress she'd made with Marc these past two days at the clinic—which was very little if his permanent scowl was any indication of it—would be completely unraveled if he caught wind of this innocent text exchange. One that had those pesky butterflies in Sadie's stomach practicing for a circus performance.

But she couldn't help herself. For the first time in months, she felt . . . happy.

"Starting without us?" Laurel fell into her seat and instantly pilfered a chip.

Sadie stuffed her phone in her purse, nearly dropping it on the floor. She stashed her shaky hands in her lap and hoped her sisters weren't paying attention to the blush doing its best to creep up her fair-skinned neck.

"She's been working with Marc for two straight days," Haylee said, filling the opposite high-top seat. "I'd be drinking, too."

Laurel narrowed her eyes at Haylee while the youngest Evans sibling pretended not to notice. The playful scene happened every time they gathered for Taco Tuesday. *Thank my lucky stars.* "You're not twenty-one yet."

"One month, two weeks, and three days," Haylee announced. "Not that I'm counting."

"You're *never* counting," Sadie teased as a server appeared to take a drink order and promised a refill on the bottomless chips and salsa. She was thankful for the lighthearted atmosphere. Thankful that despite how crummy a sister she'd been for so many years that she'd been able to repair enough of the damage to have these blissfully normal Taco Tuesdays twice a month.

"I haven't gotten a call that Marc's body was discovered in a dark alley," Laurel said to Sadie.

"It's taken a *lot* of restraint." She dipped a chip heavily in salsa. More than once she'd told Warren he should sell the stuff. It was *that* good. She'd even offered her marketing services to help move inventory. But he repeatedly insisted he wasn't interested in growing the restaurant beyond what it was. *Too bad.*

"Do you think you two are . . . working things out?" Laurel continued.

Sadie shared a look with Haylee, who already knew how terribly things were going. If Sadie weren't so determined to prove to her brother that she was a changed woman, she'd have walked out after day one.

Or definitely after this morning when Marc made her clean up a blowout in exam room one. Or this afternoon when Marylou laid into her about double booking an appointment. But Sadie wasn't about to admit defeat, or that she hid in the bathroom and cried after Marylou implied she was more a burden than a help. She had too much pride for that.

"I think Marc's a lost cause," Haylee offered.

"He's toughest on those he cares about," Laurel said, as if that was supposed to make it all bearable.

Sadie let out a hearty laugh. "If that's true, then *I'm* his favorite."

The three erupted in laughter as the server delivered a heaping bowl of chips along with Laurel's margarita and Haylee's Dr. Pepper. These moments gave Sadie hope. Hope that she could have the normal life she'd always wanted. That she could be a part of this family instead of the black sheep. It wasn't until Cody forced her back to Sunset Ridge nearly a year ago that she realized how far she'd strayed from the things that mattered most.

"At least you have Conner there," Laurel added.

Sadie felt a flush heat up her neck and creep onto her cheeks. With her fair skin, it was nearly impossible to hide, even with her long hair. She pulled her locks around her like a scarf. Her crush on

Conner may be growing, but it was still a state secret. One she worked diligently to keep under wraps. It could never lead anywhere, so there was no point admitting to it. Especially to her nosy sisters.

"You might want to slow down on the drink," Laurel said, using a chip to point at the half-consumed margarita glass.

"It's not the tequila." Haylee's eyes sparkled with mischief. She might be the youngest, but she was definitely the most perceptive. Even more so than Cody. She leaned over the table, dropping her voice, and said, "You *like* him, don't you?"

"No."

"You do!"

"I do *not*." How had this conversation gone sideways so quickly? One minute they were talking about her craptastic day at the clinic, the next she was brought in for questioning about matters that shouldn't even exist. She stared at her margarita wondering if it were to blame for this mess. It weakened her usually tough armor and made her much too transparent for her liking.

"You like Conner?" Laurel repeated.

Sadie narrowed her eyes at both sisters as a few heads turned toward their table. Had she known this was going to happen, she would've picked a table in a dark corner instead of the middle of the restaurant. "You two want to say that a little *louder?*" The last thing she needed was a rumor floating around town. If Marc heard about this crush from some curious citizen during an exam, he'd fire her on the spot.

"You do!" Haylee at least had the decency to whisper her declaration. She covered her mouth with both hands, but it did little to hide the glow in her excited eyes.

"I don't *want* to."

"Why not?" Laurel asked.

Sadie stared at her for several beats, wondering if her sister was pulling her leg or genuinely clueless. "Do you want *me* to be the dead body in a dark alley?" Even if Marc had never warned her to stay away from Conner—which he had *many* times— Sadie would never intentionally be so foolish.

"Oh. *Oh.*" Realization dawned in Laurel's expression, followed by pity. "Oh, sweetie."

"Don't," Sadie hissed. There was nothing she hated more than pity. She didn't need it. Didn't deserve it. Didn't want anything to do with it. She was a big enough person to admit her screwups and own them. She wouldn't turn down some compassion. But pity? Nope. Not a chance. "It's a stupid crush. It'll go away."

"When?" Haylee chimed in.

"If I knew you two were going to gang up on me, I would've stayed home." Which was a lie. Sadie would be at the family store, working on her secret marketing campaign. One she hoped to reveal to her siblings later this week. If it worked, it could convince her parents not to sell. Or so she hoped. But she needed everyone on board. Especially since none of them were supposed to know her dad had feelers out there for an interested buyer. She'd never cared much for Evans' Outfitters until the past year when she made an effort to be a part of the place. She admired what her parents had built nearly from scratch. "What are you both doing on Thur—"

"We want you to be happy," Laurel said honestly, ignoring her attempt to change the subject. "After that whole mess with—"

"Don't say his name," Haylee warned. *Wise sister.*

"After that mess," Laurel corrected, "you deserve someone good. Someone who will make you feel like you're the sun, the moon, and the stars."

Sadie rolled her eyes. "I see the newlywed phase hasn't worn off yet." Secretly, she envied Laurel. It didn't matter that she and Chase had been apart five years before they found their way back together.

They were sickeningly sweet. The epitome of a romance novel couple. Beautiful, intelligent blonde knockout and the smoldering, kindhearted deputy fire chief. Add in their cute-as-a-button son, Eli, and adorable pup, Zeus, and they were practically a fairy-tale come to life.

Sadie wasn't foolish enough to think the same fate awaited her. And definitely not with Conner. That fantasy would have to stay safely in her daydreams, thank you very much.

"I mean it," Laurel pressed on. "Your last relationship wasn't normal."

"It was a nightmare," Sadie mumbled, getting an involuntary chill. She considered telling her sisters about the text, but decided against it. If she didn't talk about it, it didn't have any power. Aaron would never come to Sunset Ridge. She'd tried to get him here enough times to know.

"Not all guys are like that."

"And not all guys are like Chase," Haylee pointed out. "You're lucky, Laurel. Face it."

"You're still young," Laurel said to Haylee. "And there's this whole matter of Melly's father—"

"Nope." Haylee held up her hand in a stop motion. The identity of Melly's father was a mystery to everyone. A secret Haylee was determined to take with her to the grave. What no one could figure out was *why*. "We agreed. That topic of conversation is banned from Taco Tuesdays. Indefinitely."

Though Sadie was relieved for the attention shift, she didn't like that it was at the expense of Haylee. *Be the better person, Sadie.* "What are you guys doing Thursday?"

"Thursday?" Laurel repeated.

"Can you make it for a family meeting?"

Laurel's expression turned serious. "What's going on? Is someone sick? Are Mom and Dad selling the house?"

"No, you worrywart." Sadie shook her head. Lowering her voice, she added, "But if we sit back and do nothing, they *will* sell the store. I have . . . an idea." It was the first she'd spoken of her plan, and that had been hard. For weeks, she'd been secretly putting together a marketing strategy that could make business boom once again, like it had in its glory days.

"Dad's never going to go for it," Haylee said as plates of tacos arrived, thanks to Sadie's forethought in ordering ahead. "He's tired. Why else do you think he wants to offload the place?"

"Dad isn't invited. Neither is Mom. This is between us siblings. Just the five of us."

"Cody won't be back by then," Laurel pointed out.

"He's calling in."

"What time Thursday?" Haylee asked.

"Nine. Right after the store closes." She felt a mixture of excitement and nervousness. If she could convince her sisters to come, they could drag Marc along. One way or another. "And I need you to bring Marc. But don't tell him this is my idea."

"He'll come," Laurel said.

Sadie let out an eyeroll before she could police it, but it got the message across.

"I'll make sure he's there," Haylee offered, picking up a taco. "He owes me. Which means, *you'll* owe me."

The last time Haylee called in a favor, it was for a night of babysitting when their mom was out of town. No one had warned Sadie that giving Melly too much sugar after dinner would result in her being awake *all* night. Or that it would be her responsibility to stay up with the diva until three a.m. when Haylee finally came home. "Fine."

They enjoyed their halibut tacos in comfortable silence, everyone focused on a different TV screen. Sadie watched the Royals take the field and wondered how Marc reacted to Boomer's Cubs bandana. She was tempted to check her phone, but if her sisters found out she was on a texting level with Conner, it would most definitely result in disaster.

"Have any luck finding a place to rent?" Laurel asked Sadie after she cleaned her plate.

"Not yet." Last Taco Tuesday, Sadie announced her intentions to finally get her own place. She'd been home a year, long enough to get on her own feet. It bordered on embarrassing that she lived with her parents, and made it harder to convince anyone it was temporary. With Mom's generous offer to all her kids that their rooms would always be available to them should they ever need them, Sadie had been a little lazy in the moving out department.

"Admit it. You like living with me," Hayley said in exaggerated sarcasm.

"A year together and you two haven't pulled out all of each other's hair," Laurel said. "I'd call that a win." She dabbed her mouth with a napkin as their server cleared their table and promised to bring one more round of drinks. Two was their unspoken limit. But Sadie was craving a second margarita a whole lot less than some strawberry cheesecake ice cream and declined.

"I only ask because I hear there's an apartment opening up at the end of the month." Sunset Ridge only had one complex of apartments. They were newer and overlooked the bay if you were lucky enough to get one on the second floor. But last Sadie knew, they had a strict policy on dogs over thirty-five pounds. Until she met Boomer, that didn't seem like a deal breaker.

"I need a place that allows dogs. Big, fluffy, over-sized lap dogs."

Haylee and Laurel both stared at Sadie.

"What?"

"I'm just shocked," Haylee admitted. "You've come home covered in dog slobber and enough fur to make a blanket the past couple of days. And now you want to adopt one?"

"That was always my plan."

"This is about Conner, isn't it?" Haylee guessed.

Inwardly, Sadie groaned. *Not this again.* She'd need to do extra yoga after this night was over. "It's about me wanting a dog. You know, for companion-ship. Protection. Need I remind you of my dating hiatus for the rest of the year?" She'd feel better with a dog of her own. One that might intimidate unwanted visitors. Maybe Boomer's twin brother. It had nothing to do with some silly fantasy of Conner and Sadie walking their duo of big, floofy goofballs along the bay walk together, night after night.

"Unless Conner starts making googly eyes at you," Haylee said playfully. "I bet you forget all about that resolution then."

Sadie fished a twenty from her purse—inadvertently noticing a couple of texts she'd missed from Conner—and slapped it on the table. She was eager to get away, if only to read those texts in peace. The butterflies floating in her stomach started to flutter, desperate to know what he wrote. Which, much to her dismay, was all the more reason to put off reading them. "Anyone want ice cream?"

"You have room for ice cream?" Laurel asked.

"You don't?" Haylee chimed in.

"There's *always* room for ice cream." She would probably regret this, but in the effort of becoming a better sister, she added, "I'm buying."

Chapter Six

CONNER

Conner pulled into the long albeit overcrowded gravel drive to Marc's log cabin style home. One tucked away by its abundant number of trees. He lived on the edge of town on two acres, but with its secluded vibe, might as well be miles away. Conner yearned for something of the same and wouldn't settle on a house until it felt right. The ones for sale in the middle of town were nice, but they didn't offer the privacy this property did.

Once parked, he stacked the covered baking dishes—courtesy of Edith, who insisted he couldn't show up empty-handed—and headed for the front door. Boomer trotted at his side, proudly wearing the Cubs bandana and swishing his tail in anticipation. Marc didn't have a dog of his own, but he assured Conner others would bring theirs. And that the food would all be stored up high on the kitchen island.

The front door opened before he could knock.

"Told you not to bring anything," Marc said, nearly cracking a smile. But not quite. Boomer seized the opportunity to wriggle his way inside. Chipper barks rang out inside, but nothing concerning.

"Edith Banks sent some appetizers along. Thought about keeping them all for myself—"

Marc took the dishes from Conner. "All right, you can come in."

From the looks of it, Conner was the last to arrive. *That* was courtesy of Detective Harlow and her irritatingly timed phone call. Almost as if she knew it'd make him late. She asked a few more questions about Veronica and whether she'd ever talked about leaving the country. Other than her hope to go to Paris for a honeymoon, he couldn't recall.

He considered ignoring the call, but he didn't need her hunting him down and creating a stir. He'd been in Sunset Ridge long enough to understand how quickly a rumor could travel and twist on its course.

Conner reached for the front door to close it, but before he was successful, Marc spoke up. "*What* is that dog wearing?"

He couldn't help the smile that tugged at his lips despite his losing the bet. He itched to text Sadie and let her know she was right. But that would have to wait. No way he was playing with that kind of fire, no matter how innocent it was intended. "He's a Cubs fan. Or are those not allowed?"

"Marc just doesn't want to admit the dog has taste!" Denver Grant called from his spot on the couch.

"What's your dog's name?" A little boy's voice rang above the comfortable chaos. Conner looked down to see little Eli Monroe standing at his feet. He'd just turned eight—they'd celebrated that milestone two family dinners ago—but often talked as if he were twenty-eight. Wise beyond his years.

"Boomer, c'mere." The pup abandoned his new playmate, Zeus, and trotted over. "Boomer, meet Eli."

Boomer welcomed the kid with a nice, sloppy full-cheek lick. Eli giggled, the sound warming his heart. Veronica had always changed the subject when they talked about kids, but Conner never doubted that he knew he wanted many; a house full of laughter just like Eli's. "Can I give him a treat?"

"No treats for Cubs fans," Marc grumbled.

"No treats?" Eli repeated, confused. He looked at Conner for clarification.

"He likes carrot sticks," Conner said, ignoring Marc as he set the appetizers out with the rest. Boomer perked instantly at hearing one of his favorite words. Conner pointed to the veggie tray. "But just one, okay? Even if he begs for more."

"Okay!"

Conner felt a hard clap on the shoulder and turned to find Chase. He'd hoped Marc's brother-in-law would be here tonight. He wanted to talk to him about becoming a volunteer firefighter. "He's a riot, isn't he?"

"Sure is."

"Sounds like we missed an interesting family dinner the other night," Chase said as he filled a plate with appetizers. Conner followed suit. "Sadie's really working the front desk of the clinic?"

"She's doing a great job."

"I'm surprised those two haven't killed each other yet."

"Is it really that bad? I only have one sister. We fight from time to time . . ." He let his comment drift on purpose, hoping Chase would fill in the blanks without additional prompt. Hoping he wouldn't sense how much Conner wanted to know what had gone down between Marc and Sadie. He wasn't supposed to care, but that ship left the harbor last night when he found her crying on that bench. When he realized just how much she was starting to mean to him.

"Something went down between them a couple years ago," Chase said noncommittally as he balanced one last pig in a blanket atop his heaping plate of food. "Laurel's told me about it, but I don't remember all the details. Something to do with her bailing at a crucial moment. Caused Marc to lose something important—"

"You two girls done gossiping?" Ford Harris called from the living room. "Game's about to start."

Seconds later, the sports announcer on Marc's seventy-inch TV screen announced the first pitch of the game. Chase and Conner filed into the living area to join the rest of the group. The U-shaped conversational sofa allowed them all—eight in total—to sit comfortably, each with their own cup holder and footrest. For as standoffish as Marc could come off, he certainly enjoyed entertaining.

Conner scanned the group, silently testing

himself on names. *Ford Harris, Ryder and Denver Grant—brothers—Liam Davies, Chase Monroe and his son Eli.* He couldn't remember what each of them did, but he was proud of himself for remembering who they were after only a short time in town.

Boomer lay at Conner's feet, peering hopefully at him. Poor guy had smelled Edith's pigs in a blanket the whole drive over. Even if they were as good as currency here, Conner couldn't resist those puppy-dog eyes. He broke off part of a mini hot dog and held it out for the pup as Marc settled into the seat next to him.

"Long week, huh?" Marc said.

"Yeah." If all Conner had in his life was the clinic chaos, the statement would still ring true. "Nothing we can't handle, though."

"I'm certainly glad you're here," Marc said, his focus on the screen. Compliments or expressions of gratitude were not among his strong suits. Never had been in the years Conner'd known him. It meant a great deal to hear him say so.

"It all worked out the way it was supposed to, I'd say." Conner hadn't gone into detail about his failed engagement. Marc wasn't the chit-chatty type for that conversation to have happened at length. But he knew enough. Hopefully, whatever Detective

Harlow was trying to dredge up wouldn't force Conner to be more forthcoming. He didn't relish the idea of reliving that humiliation a second time around. But after his talk with Sadie last night, one that revolved around lies, he was already contemplating filling Marc in so he wouldn't be blindsided in the event the detective made trouble. Even if unearned.

"Hope you're not planning to tuck tail and run after this week is over," Marc added.

"I'm not going anywhere." *Not by choice.*

"You might sing a different tune by the end of the week. Just remember, Judy's coming back Monday."

It was dangerous territory, but Conner wasn't going to stay silent. "Sadie's doing all right filling in. Especially for having no experience."

"She bothering you? Sadie?"

The question caught Conner off guard. He dropped the pig in the blanket and Boomer caught it as it rolled off the knee of his jeans. "Not at all."

"I asked her not to," Marc said, still watching the game though little was happening. The score was zero to zero and there was only one out at the bottom of the first.

Conner hadn't paid much attention to baseball

since he lost his dad more than a decade ago. The game had never been the same without him to watch it with. That the Cubs had been his team—their team—should capture some of his attention. But too much lingered on his mind. Especially when it came to Sadie Evans.

"She tends to do the opposite of whatever I ask, though." Marc twisted the cap off a bottle of beer. "Just wanted to make sure she's leaving you alone."

It wasn't Conner's place to pry. He'd reminded himself of that for weeks. But he hadn't gotten enough of an answer out of Chase, so the question slipped out anyway. "What happened between you two?" When Marc's eyes fell shut and stayed that way as he sucked in a breath, instead of apologizing for not minding his own business, Conner added, "The rest of your family seems to get along so well. It's hard not to notice the tension between you two."

"I give people a lot of chances," Marc answered, his voice low. Not that anyone else was listening. Ryder and Denver were deep in conversation at the opposite end of the couch while Liam, Ford, and Chase explained a double play to Eli. "I gave my sister more than I give most. If Judy wasn't out of town on an emergency—"

"Sadie seems to be picking it up well enough,"

Conner offered once more, treading as lightly as he could. But something inside him stirred to life. The urge to defend the bold redhead who took up residence in his thoughts more often than he'd liked to admit. He cared more than he ought to. Thought about her constantly. He told himself the picture of Boomer he sent before coming here was a check-in. A subtle reminder that he was there if things went sideways. If she were ever in any danger. He wouldn't break his promise to keep his mouth shut where her ex was concerned, but it wasn't an easy feat. If Marc only knew what was really going on—

"She's smart," Marc said. "I'll give her that. She just doesn't put it to good use most of the time."

"Maybe she's changed?"

Marc pointed his uncomfortable gaze at Conner, worry etched in his stern expression. "She hasn't come on to you, has she?"

"Of course not." But that didn't stop his pulse from racing. As if he wished the answer were different. *Where is that coming from?* He blamed Edith and Katy for their overzealousness when it came to his love life. No one woman had caught even a flicker of his interest, but he knew without a doubt if he *had* to pick one, like at gunpoint, he'd pick Sadie. He didn't linger too long on the *why* of that scenario.

"You'd be wise to keep your distance. She might come off as sweet and innocent, but she tends to leave a path of destruction when she leaves. And she *will* leave. She's not fooling anyone." Marc took a pull of his beer. "I don't want you to go through some unnecessary crap because of my sister. You've been through enough."

"Have you considered—"

"Marc, where you hiding the *good* beers?" Ryder called from the opposite end of the U-shaped sofa. "I didn't see any of those in the fridge."

Marc pushed out of his seat, leaving Conner to dwell on everything he said. His warning should have no bearing on him. He had no intentions of getting involved with anyone, let alone his buddy's little sister. But he knew darn well he was fooling himself if he tried to pretend any of the protective feelings he was having toward Sadie were brotherly in nature.

They were not.

He pulled out his phone, intending to search for information on the upcoming Blueberry Festival. If his sister in Texas knew about the bachelor auction, it stood to reason it was readily available. He hated the thought of making himself a spectacle. But it *was* for a good cause. The animal shelter desperately needed some upgrades.

It had nothing to with moving on from Sadie.

There was nothing to move on from. *Right?*

Participating in the bachelor auction and agreeing to go on a date with someone else might help keep Sadie in the friend zone. Marc couldn't fault them for being friends. At least he hoped not.

Except, instead of clicking the link for information on the bachelor auction, Conner found himself texting Sadie.

Conner: How did you know?

Conner: Guess I owe you ten bucks :)

He hit send before he could delete the smiley face. What had gotten into him? He was walking a tightrope when it came to Sadie on a day-to-day basis. But texting her from Marc's place? He might as well be walking that tightrope chased by a bear breathing fire.

After waiting several embarrassing seconds for a response that didn't come, he shoved his phone back in the safety of his pocket.

"I'd offer you one—" Marc said to Conner.

"But I'm on call. All good."

"You doing that bachelor auction?" Conner asked Marc, already certain he knew the answer. "The one for charity."

Marc grumbled. "I don't want to, but considering they're raising funds for the animal shelter . . ." He finished his thought with a pull of his beer. He didn't have to say the rest out loud. Conner got it. If they opted out, it wouldn't look good. They were the local veterinarians and both single. Both great candidates to raise money for a worthwhile cause. And the only two in the room who qualified since Eli was too young.

"I'll do it if you do," Conner said, not wanting to mean it. Why did the words feel like a betrayal? *Unless Sadie makes the winning bid.* Now *there* was a thought. A date not even Marc could argue with because it was for charity. Oh, boy. He was in deeper than he thought.

Chapter Seven

SADIE

Sadie slipped on a pair of comfy flats, grabbed a backpack, and headed out the door, armed with enough leftover fettuccine alfredo to keep Conner fed for the rest of the week. If she hadn't already stuffed her face, the aroma might entice her to detour somewhere private so she could inhale a decent portion. Mom was an amazing cook. She'd miss that when she moved into her own place.

But her sisters were right: it was time.

She was twenty-six, going on twenty-seven in a matter of weeks.

Getting back on her feet was one thing. But a year later, living with her parents was now embarrassing. Add to it that she'd *kill* for a night of sleep that wasn't interrupted by Melly's cries, and Sadie was ready to pack her bags the second she found a large-dog-friendly place to rent. Melly was the cutest little girl in all the land. Unless it was two thirty in the morning and she was cranky. Then she was the world's cutest terrorist.

Plus, she could always pilfer leftovers.

Sadie opted to leave her car in her parents' driveway and travel on foot instead. Summer in Sunset Ridge was made for walking.

After chaotic day number three at the vet clinic, she craved the fresh air and easy stroll to let her nerves calm the rest of the way. Today had tested her patience. Her sanity.

First it was the angry customer who unloaded on her on the phone when she informed him she couldn't get his cat in for a routine checkup for two weeks. Then Marc's cherished coffee maker dying a slow but expected death and leaving the entire office without much-needed fuel. But the clear winner was the golden retriever puppy who lost his breakfast and then the ability to control his bladder down the front of her shirt, followed by the snide comment from her brother that receptionists weren't usually so *hands on*.

It had taken every ounce of willpower *not* to walk out the door at ten thirty. At least she'd packed a change of clothes.

The day hadn't gotten any better.

When Marc caught her offering Mom's butterscotch chip cookies to Conner—never mind she'd offered to everyone else first—he chose that moment to assign her lobby cleanup. Which, after an early afternoon downpour, was painted in muddy streaks and smelled like a hundred wet dogs.

Thankfully, the air was now crisp and refreshing, the sun warming her skin. For once, the calming technique seemed to work. Or maybe it was Alaska. She may not be an outdoorsy girl, but she could appreciate the magical qualities of nature that surrounded her within the safety of the city limits. Hard to be too Zen in the middle of nowhere knowing a bear might appear out of thin air.

She was so caught up in breathing techniques that she nearly missed Ed.

Sadie let out a tiny scream in the middle of Fireweed Lane. The casserole dish rattled in her shaky grip. She hugged it against her chest.

"We meet again," she said to the moose as she

stood in the middle of the deserted road. As much as she needed to keep her distance from Conner because her feelings were *definitely* out of control, she craved this quick meetup. One where Marc wasn't breathing down her neck to make sure she behaved. She was *not* going to lose the excuse she had to see him.

Ed tilted his head as he stared back.

"Okay, maybe *quick* is a lie. But it's not my fault he didn't tell me his dog was an Instagram celebrity." Hence the backpack filled with recording equipment to help make a couple of videos for Boomer's eager fans.

Ed snorted, and seemed to nod toward the casserole dish cradled in her arms.

"Oh, no. You are *not* getting Mom's fettucine alfredo. You'll have to trample me first." When Ed took a step forward, Sadie squeaked again. "Kidding! Kidding, Ed! Geez." She quickly scanned the neighborhood, wondering where everyone was. It was too beautiful a night to be inside. Unless they were secretly recording her for TikTok. *Not* the way she wanted to be remembered should this all end badly.

Sadie's heart raced as the two remained in a standoff.

She was only two blocks from Conner's place.

But unless she wanted to backtrack and take a very long detour, she was stuck waiting this out.

"Where is your *girlfriend*, Ed?" The moose seemed to perk at that. Well, maybe he did. Maybe she imagined it. After the agonizingly long day, she was probably hallucinating. "Should we expect to see moosettes any time soon? Or did your relationship end up in the toilet like mine?"

Ed snorted, as if he resented that comment. Or it might mean he was getting annoyed with the human taunting him from the middle of the residential street. Sadie hugged the casserole dish tighter. At least this time she was wearing semi-practical shoes if the need to run arose.

"I take it back, okay? I bet you have a wonderful . . . moose wife."

Ed lifted his head and Sadie swore she caught a smile. She squinted her eyes shut hard and reopened them. She needed a good night's sleep worse than she needed her next breath. She was seriously seeing things. Delusional things. Moose didn't smile. They didn't find a mate for life like penguins or wolves. They were loners outside of rutting season.

"Can I *please* pass?"

When the moose trotted down the street, away from her, she stood dumbfounded. No way he'd understood her. That wasn't possible. But her head hurt too much to worry about what was possible and not anymore.

She waited until Ed was several yards down Fireweed Lane before she dared to cross the street. She was only half a block further when she spotted Marc's truck turning a corner and heading out of town. Her heart leapt into her throat, realizing her brother had likely been at Conner's place. The brother that would kill her deader than dead if he thought she was trying to spend time with his best friend.

"Ed?" she whispered, automatically looking over her shoulder despite the fact that he was no longer visible. "I'm going crazy."

Maybe it was a sign she should turn around and go home. Tell Mom Conner wasn't home or just stop somewhere and stuff her face so she could bring back an empty casserole dish. Instead, her feet shuffled toward her original destination. Tempting fate. Sadie walked slower as she got closer, watching diligently for Marc's truck in case he decided to return. She could explain away the leftovers, but not the video equipment.

She caught a glimpse of Boomer in the front window and instantly her tension left her body as he perked at spotting her. One ear popped to attention while the other remained limp. He let out a deep bark that fit his name. She hardly rang the doorbell before the front door opened.

"Sadie, hi."

At the sight of Conner, she forgot how to speak. Words? What were words? Nothing important when you were faced with six foot two or three of delicious man. Conner was missing a shirt, which answered her question about washboard abs—*yes, he had six. Maybe eight. Count later, Sadie*—and his hair was tousled as if he'd just woken from a nap. Though with Marc having just left, it might've been a workout that caused the chaos. Then there was that beard of his, a day past needing a trim, practically calling her fingers to comb through it. Would it tickle her skin if they kissed?

"That smells great!"

She let out a sigh of relief that he spoke again during her stupor, easing her embarrassment away. *Focus, Sadie. Stop drooling!* "Mom wanted to make sure you were fed." No way was Sadie admitting this was her idea. She was smarter than that. "Ed nearly ran me over for it, so I hope you appreciate every last bite."

"Ed?" He shook his head as Boomer wedged his

way around Conner's legs and stared up at Sadie. "Let me take that before someone causes a catastrophe." The brush of his fingers as Conner pilfered the casserole dish caused Sadie's bones to melt. Every single one. At this embarrassing rate, she'd never survive a kiss. Not that she had any intentions of kissing him during her year of being single. But she wouldn't exactly fight one off if Conner Michaelson wanted to offer one up. "Come in," he said. "Please."

Sadie had two options: head to the store to work on her marketing plan she was due to present to her siblings tomorrow night, or accept his invitation, knowing her heart might not make it out in one piece. Or least, not entirely belonging to her anymore.

She stepped inside.

"You didn't tell me Boomer was an Instagram sensation," she said as she closed the door behind her, officially sealing her escape route.

"I didn't mention that?" he asked, feigning innocence.

"You also didn't mention that you don't know how to make reels."

"What makes you think that?"

She followed him into the kitchen, desperately trying not to stare at his shirtless torso as he proceeded to scoop a large portion of pasta into a bowl. He didn't bother heating it, and stuck a fork in the lukewarm meal. "Because your fans—or should I say *Boomer's* fans—basically beg for video clips every time you post a new photo." She let the backpack fall from her shoulders. "I thought I could help."

"Help?"

"Make videos. Reels. You know, those pictures that move and have sound?"

Boomer looked back and forth between Conner with his dinner and Sadie with the mysteries she was extracting from her bag and placing on the island counter. She could sense Conner's hesitation. At any moment he could shut this down and send her on her way. It shouldn't bother her, but for reasons she was beyond trying to understand, she wanted his buy-in. Not approval. She was done searching for approval from anyone, especially a man.

"You know how to do all that?"

"Of course."

She wasn't active on her own accounts anymore because she didn't want Aaron to know anything about her life. But she made videos and reels for her friends in Anchorage to help them grow their small businesses. Well, the friends she hadn't lost during her embarrassing throw-herself-at-the-boss disaster.

"I think it's a great idea—"

Before Conner could get the *but* out, they heard a knock at the door.

Sadie froze, terrified Marc was back for a forgotten wallet or because his Spidey sense warned him she was deliberately ignoring his warning to steer clear of Conner. With a counter full of video equipment, it wouldn't be so easy to get out of this one. Conner pulled on a shirt—*too bad*—and went to answer the door.

"Edith, are you ready for our walk?"

Sadie's sigh of relief was loud enough to alert Boomer. He licked her wrist before he trotted over to greet their newest visitor. "Sadie, nice to see you," the elderly woman said, sounding as if she meant it.

"Hi, Mrs. Banks."

"Oh, Edith, please." She rubbed Boomer gently behind the ears. "Conner, I hope you won't mind. I think I'm going to skip our evening walk. I thought I was up to it, but my hip is cranky. I think there's more rain on the way."

Sadie did a discreet once-over, noticing the older woman's sneakers and light jacket. She was clearly interrupting a routine.

"Are you sure? We were just about to invite Sadie to join us."

Why was she fighting this crush again? Oh, yeah. The threat of certain death. "I love walks," Sadie chimed in.

"Then you two go." Boomer let out a small groan, apparently at being left out. "You *three* go. Excuse me for misspeaking, Boomer." Conner tried to convince Edith to tag along, promising they could take things slow. But at the end of it, Edith waved her goodbyes. A few steps from the front door, she looked over her shoulder and said, "Midnight fishing."

"Midnight fishing?" Sadie repeated, waiting for Conner to explain.

Instead, he shrugged. "No clue."

"I don't believe you."

"You up for a walk?" Boomer started pacing, his tail swishing in excitement. "You can record some footage while we're out."

Sadie's heart pounded against her ribcage. How stupid would it be for them to be seen in public together, just the two of them? Marc wouldn't buy that Boomer counted as a chaperone. If she were smart and not being led by the part of her that craved his presence, she'd go home. But that's not what she did. "A walk sounds great."

"Let me grab my shoes."

Boomer danced around in excitement, running back and forth between them. "You sure love your walks, huh, buddy?" She squatted to give him a big hug, giggling when he licked her cheek. "You really are the best, aren't you? Don't suppose you have a brother I can adopt?"

"I don't know if Boomer has siblings," Conner answered from the recliner as he tied his shoes. "I found him in a drainage ditch during a thunderstorm. He was half starved and covered in more mud than the lobby was today."

"Oh, boy. That's a lot of mud."

"You're telling me."

"So, you rescued him?" Heart. Officially. Melted.

"I think he really rescued me. I found him the day I broke things off with my ex." He spoke so easily about his past, as if the sting no longer gutted him. Sadie envied his ability to move on. Or maybe he was compartmentalizing. Either way, she would happily take a lesson or two from him.

"No one needed me anymore," he went on as they headed out the back door and waited for Boomer to get the zoomies out of his system. "My mom got remarried and had someone to fix the leaky sink faucet and clean out the gutters. My sister met an amazing guy and now they're planning their wedding. He helps her through her anxiety attacks now."

"That's how you knew what to do," Sadie said in more of a whisper. But Conner seemed to hear her anyway.

"I wouldn't wish those on anyone."

"Yeah, they suck."

"I tried to find Boomer's owners, but he didn't have a chip. After three months of posting his picture everywhere, I gave up the search. Decided we were meant to be." He whistled for Boomer and held up the leash. The dog raced across the yard at lightning speed and assumed the position, offering up his collar.

"I think it was meant to be."

Conner turned his attention to Sadie, making her feel all kinds of vulnerable with those intense brown eyes boring into her. "You can call me, okay?" He reached for her hand and gave it a gentle squeeze, effectively rendering all of her brain cells useless. "You don't have to go through those alone. I *want* to help."

Her first instinct was to ask why, but she didn't let it leave her lips. She was quickly learning Conner was the generous kind of man who'd give a stranger the shirt off his back and never expect anything in return. His giving nature could equally rival her selfish one. Did they get any more opposite than that?

"Hey," he said, suddenly standing close to her on the deck. Or had he been standing that close all along? Around him, reality was a blur at best. Sadie felt the heat of him radiate and warm her skin as her pulse jumped. "I mean it, Sadie."

"I don't deserve that." The words escaped as a whisper, mostly because her focus kept moving to his lips. Her brain was malfunctioning because the only coherent thought rolling around inside was one that involved a forbidden kiss and whether it'd make her toes curl like it did in all those romantic comedies.

For one solitary moment in time, she swore he felt it too, the pull between them. The crackling attraction. The burning desire to stop pretending they didn't feel something for one another. That he might actually see her as more than Marc's little sister. He reached his thumb to her cheek, dragging it softly across her skin. Her entire body erupted in delightful shivers. "Don't ever let anyone convince you that you aren't worthy."

Captivated by his brown eyes that reminded her of melted chocolate sprinkled with gold flecks, Sadie forgot how to breathe. *Omigod. It's going to happen. He's going to kiss me.*

Boomer chose that moment to wedge himself impatiently between them and bark. "All right, all right. We're going, buddy," Conner said with an easy laugh as he hopped off the deck, acting as though nothing had nearly transpired between them. If he felt even half of what she felt, his carefree smile didn't betray it.

Heart still in her throat, Sadie forced a smile of her own. "Let's get your subscribers some videos."

Chapter Eight

CONNER

Knowing Marc would be in early to go over the books and inventory as he always was on Thursdays, Conner made a point to meet him at the clinic before anyone else showed up. The conversation would be uncomfortable to say the least, but he decided it was necessary. He'd rather relive humiliation than have his pride bite him on the bum.

"You got the coffee pot working," Conner said, impressed.

"She's still got a few good years left in her." Marc poured himself a cup then offered one to Conner, who declined. "You're early."

"Wanted to clear the air about something."

"This about Sadie?"

Conner's pulse shot off the charts in a millisecond as he wondered what Marc knew. Would he really be upset about them walking Boomer together? Or had he discovered that she was at his house until the midnight sun dipped below the horizon, filming videos and voice-overs? "No, it's not about her."

"Mom said she was out late. Just wanted to make sure she wasn't bothering you."

Why did Marc always jump right to Sadie? Though tempted to press, he saved that conversation for another day. It was impossible to deny that he was developing feelings for Marc's sister. Ever since he recognized that she meant more to him than a mere acquaintance, those feelings had been growing at an alarming rate. He almost *kissed* her last night. Had thought about it every minute since. He could no longer lie to himself about how he felt about Sadie Evans. She was capturing his heart, and there wasn't much he could do to stop it.

But he'd pick that battle with Marc another day. Preferably after Sadie was through helping at the clinic so Marc couldn't use it as an excuse to fire her.

"This is about my . . . past." Conner rubbed the

back of his neck hard enough to cause pain and pulled his fingers away.

"Everything okay?"

"I gave you the highlight reel. But in case trouble stirs up, I need to give you the unabridged version." Conner followed Marc into his office and closed the door. He waited for his friend to get in a strong sip of coffee before he dove in. He told Marc about how Veronica had showered him with expensive gifts for Christmas last year. The kind that most people couldn't afford. Definitely not ones in their budget. How when he asked her where she got the money, she tried to convince him she'd won a small jackpot.

"A jackpot?"

"That was one of the lies she cooked up. Several others followed until she finally admitted the truth."

"She stole from the children's charity?"

"The same one she'd worked for going on two years. They had outstanding bills to pay to cover the cost of gifts they purchased for kids after toy dona-tions were exhausted. Without the money she stole, they weren't able to cover those bills." Conner explained how he insisted she return the personal gifts and pay back the money to the charity. That if she did, she might avoid jail time.

Veronica insisted the gifts were nonrefundable

and offered to pawn them. But it wouldn't be enough by half to cover what she'd taken. With only the money for a plane ticket home to Connecticut in her bank account, he made a bargain. Because selfishly, he wanted her gone. "I gave her a choice. She either went to the board and confessed what she'd done and let them decide her fate or I would call the cops and report her."

"You're the one who footed the bill, weren't you?" Marc guessed.

"They agreed not to press charges after I offered to make a donation to cover the losses. To be clear, I didn't ask that of them. I wasn't trying to bribe them. I wrote the check and told them they could do whatever they wanted with her. I think they let her off the hook because it was the day after Christmas."

"Is someone trying to drag your name through the mud for this?"

"I don't know," Conner admitted. "I thought it was all behind me. I haven't spoken to her since that day. I dropped her off at the airport and that was it." He told Marc about the detective, now in Anchorage, calling and asking questions about her. Eluding to the idea that she may have struck again and might be trying to take him down with her. "Maybe nothing will come of it," Conner said, hoping he was right. "But in case it does, I wanted you to hear this from me."

"Thanks. I'm glad you told me."

Conner felt a weight lift, and was not nearly as embarrassed as he'd expected. If only he could muster the same courage to talk about Sadie. About his interest in dating her. He almost kissed her last night, right there on the back deck for who knew how many neighbors to see. *In due time.*

"Anything else?"

"I'm heading to the animal shelter an hour early today," he said, standing. Saving the hardest conversation for another time. One when Sadie wouldn't be at the front desk and an open target. "A box of kittens was dropped off last night. Going to get them checked out before I get to the regularly scheduled programming."

Marc nodded and returned his focus to his computer, Conner's signal to leave him be.

He closed the door behind him and nearly collided with Sadie in the process. Her lavender scent rushed his senses, temporarily making him forget where he was. Reminding him of their intimate moment on the deck last night. It was only Marylou's voice beckoning from the front that pulled him back to reality so quickly.

"Hey!" Her voice squeaked a bit as a cute blush crept onto her cheeks. She instantly shuffled backward, holding up a covered container. "Mom made sticky rolls. They're to *die* for. Want some before I offer them up to Marc? He'll inhale them all."

"Sure," he said, following her to the break room. It was curiosity that got him more than his stomach. "What are you buttering him up for?"

"Who?"

"Marc."

"Oh. I noticed your website is outdated. I mentioned it to Marylou yesterday, but she said Marc handles all that stuff. Meaning he outsources it, I'm sure." She shoveled a pile of gooey rolls onto a paper plate and handed it over with a plastic fork. "I thought I could refresh it. Give it a small facelift and change out Doctor Morrison's photo and bio with yours. I think it's time, right? He's only been retired for months. Do you have a headshot I can use?"

Oh, boy. He was *definitely* in trouble.

"Conner?"

"Yeah."

"Yeah?"

"I have a photo and bio. I'll email it to you."

She plated another set of sticky rolls and took a deep breath. "Wish me luck."

"You don't need it." He was definitely flirting. Not that he meant to. It just happened naturally around her now. He yearned to prolong the conversation, even if for a minute. "Did he tell you he signed up for the bachelor auction?"

Sadie stopped halfway to Marc's office door. "You're kidding."

"I did too." He regretted the application the second he hit *send* yesterday. But he couldn't back out now. Better that Sadie find out from him than at the festival when she discovered him on stage. With any luck, maybe she'd bid on him. Maybe Marc wouldn't slug him if she won. One could hope.

"Oh." Her expression morphed from happy to confused to unreadable all in two seconds. "It's for a good cause. That animal shelter needs some renovations for sure." With that, she turned her attention to Marc's office door and dared a knock. Conner took it as his cue to be anywhere else.

Within minutes, his day was underway with his first patient, a husky lab mix in need of his first official checkup. Conner recognized the one-year-old pup from the shelter and was happy to see he'd found a home with two other dogs to help burn his excessive amounts of energy.

His day moved from one appointment to another

in a blur. A cranky Siamese with a lot to say about the medicated eye drops Conner prescribed. A cocker spaniel with a strong dislike for the cone of shame that nearly lost Conner a finger. An overly dramatic corgi who wanted the entire town to think he was dying during a routine nail clipping.

When a break for a late lunch finally arrived, Conner realized he only had half an hour until he needed to leave for his shift at the local shelter. He should warm up the leftover fettuccini alfredo and eat it in his office. Instead, he slipped out up front to ensure Sadie received his headshot for the website. Never mind the emailed *thanks* with a smiley face she'd sent him hours ago.

"I think I can confidently leave for lunch and not have a panic attack while I'm gone," Marylou said, flashing Sadie an actual smile as she pulled on her jacket. "Don't tell Judy, but I might actually miss you next week."

Conner waited until the coast was clear before he came out of his hiding spot. "How's the website update coming?"

Sadie visibly jumped in her chair before she spun around at him. "Were you a ninja in another life?"

"I like to think so. A pirate in another. I always

thought it would be fun to sail the seven seas searching for treasure."

"You mean robbing and pilfering riches from other ships?"

"When you put it that way . . ." He could get used to this. So easily. *Too* easily. "Did Marc grant you full access to the website?"

"Define *grant*." She bit down on her bottom lip as she pulled up a webpage that featured his head-shot and bio. As well as a brand-new background color and upbeat theme. Even the font seemed happier than the old version. "He gave me the login info."

"This is really good, Sadie."

"You think so? I wish there were photos of the animals. I could post them on social media. Or at least with customer reviews. Marylou said you guys don't even send an email survey after visits. I mean, it's not like you *need* more business. You have almost more than you can handle. But still."

"You really have a knack for this, don't you?"

"For website updates?"

"For identifying areas businesses could improve their image."

"Or grow." Her radiant smile alone was worth the truthful compliment.

"Have you thought about starting your own business?"

"I'm just focused on one business right now."

"This one?" he asked, confused.

"No. This is just a little side project that I hope earns me brownie points. I need all those I can get." She glanced at the door to the back, then back to him. "I meant my parents' store. I've been working on a secret marketing plan to really make business boom like it used to. I'm not supposed to know that Dad's been quietly looking for buyers. I just can't stand the thought of him selling it. It's a family business. I bet if it was turning a higher profit like it was in its glory days, he'd hold on to it until the rest of us could decide if we wanted to continue the legacy."

For the life of him, Conner couldn't figure out why Marc didn't see this side of Sadie. The dedicated, brilliant side. He doubted Sadie realized her own massive potential, either. Did she have any clue that with enough determination she could take over the world? Yes, he was most definitely falling. How could he not?

His gaze flickered to her lips, wondering how things might be different if Boomer hadn't interrupted the moment last night.

"I called an emergency family meeting. Tonight,

when the store closes. Well, *sibling* meeting. But don't tell Marc. He'll never come if he thinks it was my idea."

"I'm sure that's not true."

"I bet you twenty bucks the moment he realizes I'm running the show, he'll try to leave."

"Bets with you are dangerous."

"Only when they concern my stubborn brother," she mumbled.

Conner only caught a glimpse at the time because the desk phone lit up with an incoming call. The orange light that revealed caller ID as well as date and time warned him he was going to be late if he didn't get a move on it. But he didn't want to leave without . . . *without what?* They weren't dating. They were friends. At work. But he wanted more. So much more.

Though Conner slipped in the back to grab his bag and truck keys without a word, he still stopped by the front desk on his way out. "Good luck tonight. I know you'll do great."

"I need all the luck I can get."

"Let me know how it goes." When she answered with a shy smile, he added, "I mean it. Text me. I want to know." He waited only long enough for her to agree before he rushed out the door.

He passed Marylou on the way to his truck and reminded her about his early departure. She thanked him with a smile. A smile that was nearly as rare as Marc's unless she was greeting patients. No doubt this pleasant change was courtesy of Sadie. She'd survived three horrendous days and on this fourth one seemed to have things figured out.

If only Marc saw her for the woman she'd become instead of holding on to some past grudge Conner'd yet to figure out. Maybe then he could broach the subject of dating her without fear of a black eye or him disowning his sister. One could hope.

Chapter Nine

SADIE

Sadie checked the PowerPoint for the fifth time since they locked the doors of Evans' Outfitters. She combed over the details of each slide, worried she'd left out something crucial. Everything had to be perfect. But her sweating palms and nervously bouncing knee suggested it was going to be a disaster.

"You brought Bonita's blueberry scones," Haylee said as she entered the open office area housed in the back of the store and helped herself to a pastry. "You must be pretty serious about this plan of yours."

"I am." Sadie looked around her sister at the doorway.

"He's coming," Haylee said about their oldest brother.

"I'll believe it when I see it."

As Laurel joined them, immediately distracted by the scones, Haylee's phone rang. "It's Cody."

Last minute, Sadie asked Cody to call Haylee's phone instead of hers. If Conner sent her a text during her presentation and Marc saw the name on her screen, he'd lose his mind. And she'd die from a variety of emotions, one of which was guaranteed to be humiliation. Not because Conner thought enough of her to talk to her outside of family dinners and the clinic. Oh, no. Marc would surely make some grandiose declaration about how she was manipulating his best friend and therefore be a terrible person.

No one knew they were on a texting level. No one *needed* to know.

"Hi, Cody!" Sadie said with a wave once Haylee switched to FaceTime and propped him on a table against a stack of unopened boxes of fishing tackle. She missed her brother's surfer boy face this week more than most when he was traveling. But she hoped he'd be proud of how well she was handling herself, especially around Marc. "How's the book tour going?" She asked both because she genuinely liked Jenna and wanted the best for her, but also because she really wanted this meeting to stay between the five of them.

"Great! She keeps selling out everywhere we go. Right now, she's grabbing coffee with the librarians she met earlier today. Guess they have a list of ideas the kids have been begging for Jenna to put in her books and wanted to share them."

"That's great."

"Everyone there?" His question implied the obvious.

"Yes," Marc answered with a scowl as he trudged through the door. He looked exhausted from the long day. One that got longer when Conner had to leave early for his shift at the shelter. Marc had the more difficult patients today. Sadie tried to help, but her attempts of all varieties were shot down left and right. Which likely set the tone for tonight.

No matter. She could handle Marc's grumpiness.

"Okay, we can get started," Sadie announced, standing and positioning the laptop so everyone could see the presentation.

"There's scones," Haylee said to Marc, pointing at the table.

Marc ignored them and plopped in an old rolling chair. The dust from years of living in the back of the store erupted around him but he didn't seem to notice as he folded his arms and looked at her as though she was wasting his time.

"Thank you all for coming—"

"Wait. *You* called this meeting?" Marc interrupted, looking at Sadie as though he was both shocked and disgusted. And about one point seven seconds from bolting.

"Yes." She stared him down, daring him to get up from that chair. She wasn't sure if he was extra irritated with her lately because she was actually doing a halfway decent job at the clinic or because he was worried she'd ruin Conner. He probably thought she was going to chase him out of Sunset Ridge. Which was just ridiculous. If anyone would end up leaving, it would be her. It was always her. "As I was saying, thank you for coming. I know it was last minute and not necessarily convenient timing—"

"Get on with it."

"Marc, knock it off," Laurel said, whapping him against the back of the head hard enough that it echoed. He leaned forward in his seat and glared at her, but didn't retaliate. He might be the oldest of them all, but Laurel was the oldest sister and wasn't afraid to go toe-to-toe when he was being unreasonable. Thank goodness for her sisters and their unspoken referee status.

"I know we're not supposed to know about Dad wanting to sell the store"—Sadie pressed on like she had in so many meetings with unruly, immature people not paying attention. This wasn't her first rodeo—"But I thought if we could help turn things around, we could convince him to keep it a little longer. At least for a few years until we can decide whether we want to take it over."

"Who?" Marc asked.

"The five of us."

"I don't want this store," he said smugly. "I have my own business."

"I didn't mean we needed to sort that out tonight. I just want to share my marketing plan for the present—"

"I don't have time for this."

Sadie pursed her lips hard enough to prevent *Old Sadie's* words from making an escape. Oh, how she wanted to tell him off right now. Let him know him *exactly* what she thought of his unnecessary pompous, smug attitude. If it weren't for catching a glimpse of Cody's face, she might not have succeeded with taking a deep breath. After a mental count to five, she refocused on the presentation and pressed on. "I did extensive research on what products are in highest demand at each time of the year. I noticed we haven't been capitalizing on those at all. We could do theme related sales and promotions for each of them to draw in more customers. For example—"

"Dad's never going to go for this." Marc stood so quickly he sent the rolling chair flying backward. It crashed against an old metal desk. "Give it up, Sadie. All your meddling's going to do is make things worse. That's all it ever does." He stomped toward the door but stopped before he pushed it open. "And leave Conner alone. I'm not going to tell you again."

Sadie glared at him hard as her heart pounded. Faintly, she heard the gentle warning in Cody's voice as he attempted to reach her. But he was in Seattle or Long Beach. Too far away to stop her. She was sick and tired of Marc treating her like she was some delinquent who was destined to screw up everything. Sadie saw red. "What is your *problem* with me?" she spat at him.

Marc had the audacity to smirk, as if he'd been expecting this moment all along. A moment his constant jabs and snide comments had set the stage for. He seemed proud of himself, and that really set her off.

"You are an unbelievable jerk! I'm a big enough person to admit I was a crappy sister. I don't deny it. But I've been working so hard this past year. I've gone so far out of my way—"

"That's just it, Sadie. One year doesn't make up for all the disasters you've caused. It doesn't prove that you won't go right back to your old habits on a dime." He folded his arms over his chest again, the smug expression making her wish she'd invested her time in kickboxing or karate instead of yoga so she could wipe that look right off his face. "Kind of like you're doing right now."

"Marc, that's not fair," Laurel said sternly.

But the other siblings were in a losing battle. This was now between the two of them.

"No. This is bigger than that." Sadie glared at him hard, proving she wasn't going to back down until he finally caved and told her what crazy terrible thing she'd done to ruin their relationship so firmly. Because with the way he was acting, there was definitely something specific he was holding a grudge over. "What is it, Marc? What did I do that made you hate me?"

"He doesn't hate—"

"You really don't know?" Marc cut off Haylee as if she weren't even in the room. He marched up to within an inch of Sadie and peered down. Anger flared in his eyes. "You really don't remember ruining my one chance at happiness?"

Sadie flinched as if she'd been slapped. Marc hadn't moved a muscle, but his words packed such a surprising punch that she nearly tripped over her own feet. "What are you talking about?"

"Rebecca."

The room went eerily quiet.

No one had heard Marc speak her name in more than three years. Not since the day she left town without any plans to return. The day she left Marc. Sadie should've realized it was the reason he was permanently grumpy. But he'd gone and screwed that up all by himself. "Are you really blaming me for the mess you caused with her?"

"I'm blaming you because the one time I needed you to help save my relationship, you bailed. You couldn't be bothered to stick around like you promised. You let her leave when I asked you to stop her. To stall her until I could get there to fix things. It was the most important favor I ever asked of you, and you flaked like you do with everything else. Because you weren't there. Instead, where did I find you? Back at Mom and Dad's packing your bags."

Sadie wobbled on unsteady legs until she sat against the edge of a desk. "I—I don't remember."

Marc let out a disbelieving laugh that chilled her to the bone. "Of course, you don't. You're too selfish to think about anyone but yourself. Always have been, always will be. You made a promise to me and then disregarded it the second you were out of my sight." His face was beet red, his breaths coming in heavy pants. "I'll never forgive you, Sadie. I'll never believe you can change. So, stop trying." With that, he turned and marched out the door.

Several uncomfortable beats of silence followed the slamming of that door.

"You okay?" Haylee asked quietly.

"Not really."

"Sadie," Cody said, drawing her attention to the phone screen. "Call me if you need to, okay?"

She nodded, already knowing she wouldn't bother him. He deserved some drama-free time with Jenna. This was the most exciting thing to happen in her career, and Sadie wasn't going to sour it with whatever was happening at home. Part of becoming a better person was figuring out how to clean up her own messes and deal with hard things on her own. Without expecting someone else to give her the answers or do the hard work.

"I guess the meeting's over," Sadie said, using a shaky hand to close her laptop. So much for the PowerPoint. She hadn't pulled up more than the opening slide. All those late nights of research were a complete waste of time.

"Do you know what he's talking about?" Laurel asked gently, touching Sadie's arm. "About Rebecca?"

"I don't." She'd been searching her memories since Marc mentioned her name, but she was coming up empty. Maybe with some yoga or meditation, she could calm down enough to search deeper. Or kick-boxing. That would certainly help her channel her frustration and figure out what on earth he was talking about. If Marc was *this* upset, surely it was there. Somewhere. "No one wants to save the store, then?"

Her attempt to deflect fell flat. Cody had already hung up. Her sisters were looking at her with a mixture of pity and confusion. As if they were trying to remember the pivotal moment in Marc's history that she'd apparently ruined. *Join the club.*

"Have you talked to Dad?" Haylee asked.

"Didn't think it would matter unless everyone else was on board."

She fished her phone out of her purse, hoping

she might have a text waiting from Conner. When there was none, she opened her Instagram app instead. She'd posted the first video of Boomer on his account last night. It was too much to hope it'd gone viral, but reading the comments from his already adoring fans might help distract her long enough to catch her breath. She was going to the shelter this weekend to adopt a dog. One decision made. Only a hundred more to sort out.

"Did you ever consider that Dad's just tired?" Laurel asked, snagging a couple of scones and wrapping them in a napkin. No doubt for Chase and Eli.

"Then why doesn't he at least *ask* us if we want to take over?"

"And who's going to run the place?" Haylee tossed in the heavy question with pro nonchalance. It weighed on Sadie just the same. She'd been wondering the same question. She loved the marketing side of things. Maybe even figuring out how things could run more smoothly. But being the one in charge? She didn't think she wanted that responsibility.

"I guess I was hoping one of you would volunteer. Or Cody."

"Me?" Haylee let out a high-pitched laugh. "I'm

not even old enough to drink. Dad's not going to put me in charge."

"Not tomorrow." Sadie let out a heavy sigh as she clicked the button to turn off her phone screen. When she was alone, she'd consider texting Conner. It didn't look like Marc was ever going to forgive her anyway so why not press down on the gas pedal when it came to Conner? The man had almost kissed her last night. She was no longer the only one stealing glances at lips. She deserved something happy in her life, right? "Sorry to drag you guys out for nothing."

"Hey, I'm not sad about the scones," Laurel said, her chipper tone meant to break the tension. "And there's enough left over to butter up Dad."

Sadie just shook her head. Without her siblings to back her up, Dad wouldn't take her suggestions seriously. He, of all people, had the biggest reason not to believe in her. He'd had to fire her—only twice because the third time she just walked out. "Yeah, that ship has sailed."

"Don't stay out too late," Haylee said, heading to the door with Laurel. "Unless it's with Conner."

"Right. Because I'm *trying* to give Marc a reason to murder me in my sleep." But Sadie was no longer convinced that Marc's disapproval was enough reason to keep her distance from Conner. The only thing holding her back now was the rift she might unintentionally create between the two friends. She didn't want that for Conner. It wasn't fair for him to become collateral damage in all this. But it didn't stop her wishing things were different. Craving his presence like a warm, fuzzy blanket after such a crappy night.

She stayed behind to pack up the scones. Before Sadie could slip her phone in her purse, the screen lit up with a text. Butterflies instantly fluttered to life, proving that not even the crappiest situations could kill them entirely. But it wasn't Conner's name on the screen.

Unknown: Keep blocking my number, Love Bug. It amuses me ;)

She dropped her phone as if it'd bitten her. It landed against the concrete floor with a thud. Her entire chest vibrated with uneasiness. She hated how easily Aaron could still rattle her after all this time. She hadn't seen him in more than a year. Why was he bothering her now? Why couldn't he just leave her alone and let her move on from that terrible time in her life? Her breathing grew shallow and strangled as her pulse went wild. And not in the good way it went wild around Conner.

Conner.

With a shaky hand, she unlocked her phone and scrolled to his contact.

Her finger hovered above the call button. There was no one else she wanted to help her through this more than Conner. No one else she trusted. The one man she truly didn't deserve. Maybe Marc was right to keep her away from him. A good, kindhearted man like Conner didn't deserve the drama and destruction that came from being involved in her life.

She locked her screen and dropped her phone in her purse.

And proceeded to have one of the worst anxiety attacks she'd had in a long time.

Chapter Ten

CONNER

Conner was at the animal shelter two hours longer than he expected. The box of kittens he'd been led to believe held six or seven ended up holding two dozen. He refused to short change any of the other animals in his care and attention simply because he had his hands full with the world's cutest and orneriest kittens.

For a solid three minutes, he'd contemplated bringing one home for Boomer. But he liked his lamps in one piece and his blinds intact.

His first urge was to text Sadie to find out how the family meeting went. He had no doubts that

Marc made things difficult, but he truly hoped Sadie accomplished what she set out to regardless. If anyone could, it was her. But his phone was filled with missed calls from Mom. Seven to be exact. The last one was from eleven minutes ago. He switched the speaker to Bluetooth and called her back.

"Conner! I was worried about you. Is everything okay?"

"Fine, Mom. I was working a shift at the shelter and it ran late—"

"Oh, thank goodness. I worry about you, you know. You're all the way in the Arctic. A bear could attack you and we might never know."

He chuckled, missing her overly dramatic nature. She'd been convinced he'd be mauled by a bear since the first day he mentioned the opportunity in Alaska. At least once a week, she reminded him about how *dangerous* the last frontier was. Never mind that she and Rodney were planning to take an Alaskan cruise next summer now that they had a good excuse. Dangers were only for non-vacationers. "Just working, Mom. Everything okay there?"

"It's your sister."

Conner bristled with concern. If her fiancé turned out to be anything other than the pleasant, kindhearted man he presented himself to be, Conner would be on the next plane to handle things. "What happened?"

"She can't stop fussing about the seating chart."

At a stop sign, Conner just sat there and stared out. He was too tired for this. "I hardly think this counts as an emergency, Mom. The wedding is months away. Whether or not I'm bringing a plus-one is completely up in the air." It amazed him how different he felt about this topic tonight than he had only a couple of days ago. Had Sadie really made that much of an impact on his otherwise hardened heart in so short a time? Enough that he was already thinking about bringing her as his plus-one?

"She has to order the tables now, you see. Whether you're bringing a date effects which size table she orders for the groomsmen."

"You're making that up so you can be nosy."

"Am not!"

"He caught you, Annie. Give it up," Rodney, Mom's new husband, hollered in the background. "Let the man get some sleep so *we* can get some sleep."

"Good night, Mom. Rodney." He ended the call before Mom could figure out another topic to keep him on the line longer. Had he known there wasn't an emergency, he would've saved that conversation for the weekend. She'd no doubt call again after she caught wind that he signed up for the charity bachelor auction.

He drove along Forget Me Not Drive, enjoying the sun dipping below the water at long last. He was so enraptured by the scene that he nearly missed the woman standing at the edge of the curb, looking as though she were going to dart in front of him. A familiar woman. "Veronica?" He slammed on his brakes hard enough to earn a honking horn behind him. But his heart was racing more from the haunting from his past than the near-accident.

He rolled his truck forward, scanning the area where he'd spotted the woman. But there was no one now.

If he had much sense, he'd head home and directly to bed. He was obviously exhausted from the long day and seeing things. Boomer occasionally forgave him for missed walks on late nights as long as he made up for it with carrot sticks and let the pup sleep with his head on the pillow. And there *would* be drool because of it.

Tonight, though, he didn't seem to have that practical sense. Restlessness pushed him through his fatigue. The urge—the *need*—to text Sadie tugged at him almost as badly as the desire to see her. If he was being honest, he was concerned not to have heard from her by now. Had the meeting gone sideways after all?

Marc was in attendance. Of course, it had.

He waited until he pulled into the driveway to shoot off a quick check-in message and then let Boomer out back to run his zoomies. After several minutes without a response, he dared to send another. Though he'd driven by the store and found the parking lot empty, it was possible the meeting was still ongoing.

Conner: Everything okay?

He didn't want to come off as smothering, but a twisting feeling in his gut told him something was wrong. It could be the ghost sighting of Veronica causing it, but just in case, he started to type out a third text. Before he could finish, she replied.

Sadie: No.
Sadie: It's terrible.

With an obnoxious yawn so loud it made Boomer bark in suspicion, Conner made the decision.

Conner: Anything ice cream can fix?

Sadie: You shouldn't want to be around me. I'll just mess up your life.

Conner: I don't believe that.

Sadie: You should. I'm bad for you.

Conner bristled, certain she was only feeling this way because her brother had gotten in her head. If it killed him, he was going to get to the bottom of this. Marc had always had a broodiness about him, even back in vet school. But he was different now. Irritable. Quicker to snap. No way this was all on Sadie, but he was certainly taking it out on her.

Conner: Ice cream helps you live longer. I saw it on the Internet so it has to be true.

He waited for two minutes with no response. Two agonizingly long minutes.

Conner: Please? Boomer needs a walk, and I might fall asleep standing up.

Sadie: Only if it's strawberry cheesecake ice cream.

Conner: Done. If we hurry, we can catch Glacier Ice Creamery before it closes.

Sadie: Ok. Meet you there.

After changing out his work shoes for tennis shoes, Conner clipped Boomer's leash onto his collar. They only had three and a half blocks to go, but he picked the pace up to a jog to ensure he'd make it on time. If Sadie was late, he wanted to ensure she had her ice cream. She obviously needed it.

Conner could see the line was winding down through the glass-front windows as he and Boomer turned the last corner. Sadie sat on a bench, looking more fragile than he'd ever seen her. His heart ached for her. "All right, Boomer. You know what to do."

The pup wagged his tail in earnest, clearly understanding his mission.

"You got here fast," Conner said as they met Sadie at the bench. She started to stand, but Boomer climbed onto the bench and weighed her down with his upper body. *Best. Dog. Ever.*

"I was just down the block."

The urge to draw her into his arms overwhelmed him. Her pain radiated from her in droves. He suspected she'd had another anxiety attack—a bad one, if he was reading the signs right. The redness in her eyes. Puffy cheeks. The way she suffocated Boomer in a hug the second he was in her lap.

"I'll get the ice cream if you don't mind watching Boomer?"

She extended her hand for the leash, and he handed it over. He risked a simple embrace of their hands. Quick but enough to reassure her she wasn't in this alone. Not now. Not ever again. He was falling harder every day, whether he wanted to or not. He might as well embrace his feelings.

Conner returned with two heaping bowls of ice cream—strawberry cheesecake for Sadie as requested, moose tracks for him—and a pup cup filled with vanilla soft serve and crushed up Milk-Bones for Boomer. "We might need an extra-long walk if I give this to him," he said to Sadie.

"He's not fat. Just fluffy!"

"It's not the calories I'm worried about. It's the ice cream farts. They're lethal."

At long last, Sadie cracked a smile and started to laugh. "Boomer, they're not *that* bad, are they?"

"He can clear a room in under two seconds." Conner wriggled into the space left on the bench, which was tight with Boomer spread out. But the pup wasn't leaving Sadie, even for ice cream. Not that Conner minded the excuse to sit so close to Sadie, even with Boomer using his puppy-dog eyes to guilt Conner into bringing the cup to him.

Boomer's eyes bulged to twice their size when he got his first lick.

At Sadie's first bite, she closed her eyes and moaned in delight. Pure, unscathed happiness replaced her forlorn expression. "This hits the spot."

"I'm glad."

"Thank you," Sadie said. "For the ice cream. For . . . coming to my rescue."

"I highly doubt you need rescuing, Sadie Evans. But you're welcome anyway."

They enjoyed their ice cream in comfortable silence as the lights in the creamery behind them went dark. The last of the crowd thinned, leaving them with the faint glow of a nearby streetlight. They didn't need it. Even now, at just after eleven, a dusky light illuminated everything around them.

"Have you ever been midnight fishing?" he asked.

"Nope." She wiped a drop of ice cream from the corner of her lips, renewing his desire to kiss her. "I'm not exactly the outdoorsy type."

"But you love being outside," he observed.

"The fresh air is nice," she admitted. "But I'm too chicken to go further than an overlook in my car. Like camping? No thanks. I don't need a hungry bear licking my toes in the middle of the night, thank you very much."

Finishing the last of his ice cream, he lifted from the bench and dropped his cup in the nearby bin. "You expecting someone to dump a bunch of honey on your toes?"

"With my luck?"

He took her empty bowl from her and held out his hand for hers. She stared at it, hesitating. "If you bail on the walk now, you're taking Boomer home with you. You'll find out I'm not kidding about his ability to gas a room."

As the pup hopped up off the bench, she accepted his hand.

The very best part was that she didn't immediately try to pull it back as they strolled toward the bay. He dared to interlace his fingers with her own, only releasing a breath he'd been holding when she locked her fingers tighter around his.

"So, midnight fishing."

"What is it with you and this idea?" she teased.

"Edith's fault, really. She mentioned that she and her late husband used to do it, and I've been intrigued ever since." They crossed Forget Me Not Lane, but Conner didn't think to look for the ghost he'd seen earlier that night. He was too lost in his moment with Sadie and Boomer, committing it all to memory. Determined to create many more moments like it in the future. "Would you want to go with me? Tomorrow night?"

He knew how to fish, but didn't have any of his gear in Alaska. His poles, tackle box, and everything else necessary to pull this off was in Mom's garage, back in Houston. But he could pick up what they needed at Evans' Outfitters. He only needed her to say yes.

"What about Marc?"

"I'm going to talk to him next week. Once you're done at the clinic so he can't use that against you."

"I'm not going back."

"I don't know what happened tonight, but I really hope you'll stick it out one more day. But that's just me being selfish." He caressed the side of her hand with his thumb. "I really enjoy your company." He already mourned the days next week when he wouldn't see her at work. But her talents had potential far outside the clinic.

"I don't want to cause trouble," Sadie said, offering him a small smile. "Apparently, that's my specialty."

He pulled her to a gentle stop on the deserted sidewalk, tugging her and shuffling his feet until they faced each other straight on. He dropped Boomer's leash and caught it beneath his shoe because he needed both hands for what he was about to do. Resting one hand on her shoulder, he used the other to fully cup her cheek. When she lifted her gaze to his to prove she was truly in this moment with him and listening, he said, "You are worth every ounce of trouble. Every single one."

Leaning down, he tilted her chin up. He rested his forehead against hers, allowing their breaths to mingle. Giving her a chance to pull away. To tell him this wasn't what she wanted. Instead, she snaked her hand around the back of his neck and closed the distance with her lips.

At the first brush of their lips, he knew this kiss was different from any other he'd ever experienced. His body hummed with warmth and hope. He combed his fingers into her hair and deepened the kiss, surrendering all his fears in this moment. Their lips moved in a gentle yet hungry rhythm that drew them closer together. Sadie wrapped both arms around his neck and held on tight.

And Conner knew.

He wasn't just falling.

He had fallen.

Chapter Eleven

SADIE

Armed with Black Bear coffees for the vet techs, sticky buns for Conner, a bottle of Pure Leaf iced tea for Marylou, and a bag of the world's most boring coffee grounds for Marc's back-from-the-dead coffee maker, Sadie marched confidently toward the clinic's front door. Whatever storm waited for her inside, she was facing it head on.

After Marc slammed the door at the end of their meeting last night, Sadie was convinced she'd never step foot in the vet clinic again. But Conner . . . She sighed so happily she thought it might make her weightless and lift her off the ground. Conner restored her waning confidence. Maybe it was his words—or maybe that amazing kiss that was indeed toe-curling—that renewed her determination and gave her the courage to face her brother once more. Or maybe it was her sheer stubborn stupidity that convinced her to show up and risk poking the grizzly bear that was Marc.

"Marc said you weren't coming in today," Marylou said in pleasant surprise as Sadie fished the bottle of iced tea from her tote bag and handed it to Marylou.

"He didn't think I'd show up," Sadie admitted, shrugging her shoulders as if indifferent. But she was far from it. She'd been awake hours after Conner walked her home, tossing and turning. Both reeling from that kiss and searching her memories for the single event that caused Marc to lose all faith in her.

At 3:42 a.m., the same time Melly woke the house with an ear-splitting scream, Sadie finally remembered.

"I'm glad you're here," Marylou said honestly. "And the website facelift looks great. Too bad we can't keep you around when Judy comes back. I bet the three of us would be a powerhouse team."

Sadie's heart actually melted at the compliment, and happy tears threatened to leak from the corners of her eyes. She'd been working so hard to prove herself this past year, convinced it would never be enough, that Marylou's compliment was as good as a Boomer hug. Well, *almost*. Nothing was quite as good as those. "I'm happy to fill in when one of you needs a vacation," Sadie offered.

"I'll keep that in mind."

Sadie didn't make it to the door to the back before it burst open.

"What are you doing here?" Marc narrowed his cold, icy gaze at her.

"Following through with my commitment." Her words were stern. They had to be to get through to Marc. He wasn't the kind of guy who went soft at a sign of weakness. "I promised to stay through Friday. Unless Marylou wants tomorrow morning off. Then I'll cover through Saturday."

"Haven't you caused enough trouble?"

"Knock it off with the grumpy attitude. You kick her out today, you might as well take a seat up here yourself, doc," Marylou scolded like a mother.

"Fine," Marc relented. Though it was likely only to appease Marylou, Sadie took the win. She owed Marc an apology, but she didn't want to do it out front with witnesses.

"Did you see the website?" Marylou asked Marc. "Sadie did a great job!"

Marc folded his arms over his chest. "I thought you were just updating the staff page."

"If you don't like what I did, you can put it all back."

"No, you won't," Marylou said. "Patients can actually find the information they're looking for now. Half a dozen said so only yesterday. Do you know how many phone calls she's already saved me?"

Marc responded with a grumble before he disappeared in the back, allowing Sadie to finally relax. She'd expected a confrontation when she showed up this morning, but she was glad it was over. "Let me drop this stuff off in the break room. I'll be right back."

She left the coffees for the vet techs, hearing their praises from across the room as they prepped for the busy day ahead, and delivered the Tupperware container of sticky rolls to Conner's office, resisting the urge to shut the door and steal another toe-curling kiss. But the vet techs would no doubt find that suspicious, even if she and Conner hadn't specifically talked about keeping things neutral at work. Which they had last night as he walked her home, holding her hand the whole way.

"You're trying to fatten me up for this auction," Conner teased, that megawatt smile awakening every single butterfly in her tummy. Of which there were apparently millions. Her lips buzzed with the memory of the magical kiss that'd left them both breathless. Never in her life had a kiss made her feel that way.

That's how she knew this was different.

"Maybe I just don't want too much competition," she teased.

"Still on for"—he lowered his voice to a whisper—"tonight?"

She nodded, unable to keep a giddy smile from stretching her cheeks. "Okay, I have to talk to Marc. Again." With a deep breath, she forced herself into action before her nervous thoughts could talk her out of it.

The old Sadie would've run at the first sign of an uncomfortable confrontation where she was at fault. Put up a bratty front to hide her embarrassment until she was alone and could wallow in self-pity.

Those days were officially over.

For good.

Sadie knocked on Marc's door and waited for his gruff, "Come in."

"I brought you a coffee refill." She held up the bag of generic, store-brand dark roast grounds.

Marc started to say something, but stopped. He was out of coffee, and he knew it. A snide remark might cost him. Sadie took advantage of this rare moment of his silence to slip inside his office and close the door behind her. She set the bag on his desk and looked him square in the eyes, forcing herself to push through the uneasy, squirmy feelings doing their best to activate her flight instincts.

"I'm sorry."

The slightest hint of surprise flashed across his face, but his mask was up just as quickly. "For what?"

"About Rebecca."

His dark eyes clouded over. "I'm not talking about this. I'm at *work*, Sadie."

"I didn't remember last night. But I do now." Her breath was unsteady, but she kept focusing on it anyway. Starting her count to ten so many times because she kept losing track somewhere after four. "I went to the pier that day, like you asked. She wasn't there. She was already gone."

Marc folded his arms over his chest. "I don't believe you."

"I went straight there, like you asked. I looked for

her, but I didn't see her. Marc, I swear if I knew what *not* finding her meant to you, I would've done everything I could to track her down." The words weren't true, and she hated that. "Okay, that's a lie. Old Sadie would've tried a little harder, but not hard enough. Maybe I would've found her if I'd known, but let's face it. Probably not. I was a crummy sister, friend, and overall person for more years than I like to admit."

She didn't bother telling him about Aaron. How after she went to the pier and didn't find Rebecca, Aaron sent her a text begging her to come back to Anchorage right away. He *had* to see her. They were in the early, honeymoon phase of their relationship. The one where she was convinced nothing could go wrong. The one where she ignored every red flag. Though looking back, she recognized them in spades.

She kept it all to herself because Marc didn't condone excuses.

"It's too late, Sadie. I told you that."

"I don't believe that." She'd already formulated a plan to make this right, but she wouldn't breathe a word of it to Marc until she knew she could pull it off. She didn't want to put him through any more grief where Rebecca was concerned. "We're family,

Marc. Like it or not. You're stuck with me in your life because I'm not going anywhere. Sunset Ridge is my home. It's where I want to stay."

"And what?" Marc scoffed, leaning back in his chair. "Take over the family store?"

Her heart still ached at how easily her siblings had abandoned her last night, but she pushed the thoughts away to deal with another time. "I've changed, Marc. I've worked really, really hard to grow up and face reality. I've owned up to my mistakes. I'm sorry I didn't know what you were talking about last night. If I knew that's why you hated me so much, I would've made that right on day one of becoming a better person."

"I don't *hate* you."

Sadie gasped, shocked at the words that were nearly as good as an admission of love.

A knock at the door reminded Sadie this was a place of business. "Can we talk more later?"

"Maybe."

Sadie did the most daring thing she'd done in a long time when it came to Marc. She attacked him with a bear hug. "Thank you." She made her escape before he could growl at her. Maybe things could work out after all.

With her and Marc.

And with Conner.

"You actually *hugged* him?" Haylee asked with a disbelieving laugh from across the booth at Willamina's Big Dipper. She let out a big, dramatic yawn. Thanks to Melly, Sadie wasn't the only one losing sleep in that house. "I would've paid money to see the look on his face. Marc doesn't do hugs."

"I caught him by surprise. Doubt I'd get away with it again. But it's real progress," Sadie said proudly. "I mean, he's a *long* way from forgiving me. But until this morning, I really didn't think that day would ever come."

Willamina stopped by their table to check on them and offer both soup and coffee refills. Haylee held up her empty mug. "The stronger, the better. This mama is exhausted." She turned her attention to Sadie once her cup was refilled. "I hope you appreciate me giving up my precious naptime for this lunch."

"You're eating for free."

"Wait until you have kids someday. You'll understand how valuable naps are. Especially when your kid thinks it's funny not to sleep through the whole night. Or, you know, like any of it." Haylee took a sip of her coffee and seemed to semi come back to life. "Or are you still convinced you're never going to have kids and just be an auntie?"

"I don't know," she said honestly.

"Whoa." Haylee sat up straight and stared uncomfortably at Sadie. "You're really falling for him, aren't you? Like this isn't just some little crush anymore."

Sadie wouldn't be able to hide her giddy smile if she tried, so she didn't bother. "Can I tell you a secret?"

"Well, duh."

"I'm serious!"

"So am I. Spill it. Are you two planning to secretly elope in Cancun?"

Not yet. Sadie leaned over the table and lowered her voice. "Conner kissed me last night."

Haylee threw both hands over her mouth, apparently too stunned for words. But her wide eyes implied a number of possible reactions—shock, confusion, mortification.

"You can say something," Sadie hissed quietly.

"I'm just so . . . shocked."

"Why?" Sadie couldn't help the squeeze of insecurity that admission gave her tattered heart. One that was well on its way to healing, but still plenty vulnerable nonetheless. She was afraid whatever was transpiring with Conner was too good to be true. A little reassurance that it wasn't would be nice. "Is it so hard to believe that he likes me?"

"Of course not," Haylee said, dumping a creamer packet in her half-consumed coffee. "I'm just surprised because I didn't know you guys were on that level. You went from a crush you didn't want to have to kissing the man. That's a big gap that I apparently missed out on." She raised an eyebrow at Sadie, the simple gesture demanding details.

"Marc doesn't know."

"You think that's wise?" Haylee tilted her mug up to her lips, emptying it. She frowned at the mug and shoved it off to the side of the table. "I mean, after last night—"

"I apologized to him. This morning."

Haylee stared at her as though she'd grown a second head. Maybe even a third. "Who are you and what have you done with my bratty sister? She's a redheaded pain in the—"

"I remembered what happened." Sadie stared into her soup bowl, using her spoon to chase chunks of carrots. Willamina's soup was not only delicious, it was legendary. People came from all over the state to try it. But she wasn't all that hungry. "I found Rebecca. On Facebook."

Slapping her hand against her forehead, Haylee shook her head. "First of all, I thought you were off Facebook. You know. Because of Voldemort's twin brother. Second, leave this alone. You think Marc's mad now. Just . . . don't go poking a stick into a hornet's nest. Or you know, into the belly of an angry grizzly bear."

Before Sadie could admit she already sent a message, her phone pinged with an incoming email. She'd changed the tone last night to keep the sound from instantly turning her blood cold. Eventually, she needed to change her number again. But she didn't want to admit to her family why. Admitting it to Conner had been hard enough, even as easy as he seemed to make everything. The task could wait a few more days. At least until after the news about her unexpected relationship with Conner—or whatever they were—was public knowledge. "It's from the apartment complex," she told a nosy Haylee who was leaning far over the table to see. No doubt expecting some lovey-dovey text from Conner to spy on.

"And?"

Last night, somewhere between the hours of one

thirty and two thirty, Sadie decided to contact the apartment complex to see if they'd be willing to make an exception for a large breed dog. The open unit was on the second floor and offered a killer view of the bay. It wouldn't last long. She'd been saving for months and had the deposit ready to put down. But she didn't want it if Boomer couldn't visit. Or if she couldn't adopt a brother for him to play with.

"They recently changed their policy!" Sadie gushed.

"And?"

"They don't have a weight restriction anymore." She set her phone on the table and looked at her sister. "Want to help me pick out a dog from the shelter this weekend, after the Blueberry Festival's over?"

"You're serious."

"Yes!"

"Did you get the apartment, then?"

"I'm going to fill my application out after lunch." Wait. New Sadie didn't worry about personal business on her brother's dime. Well, not exactly *dime* considering her offer to work for free and his definite lack of mentioning a paycheck. But still. "After work. I'll fill it out after work." She reached for the check, but Haylee grabbed it from her.

"You're not the only one who can pay, you know. I *do* work."

Sadie held up her hands in surrender. "I'm not going to argue."

"Good. Because I'm totally using this to redeem a sleepover when you get moved in. One that's kid-free."

Sadie's heart was full in that moment. Not quite bursting at the seams, but as close as it'd been in a long time. How many times had she *wished* she had moments like these with her sister? Or a man in her life who not only helped her through anxiety attacks but didn't try to tell her she was faking them for attention? Even things with Marc had hope for the first time in forever. "You don't have to bribe me, you know. You can come over as much as you want."

"You think Mom would keep Melly until she's like . . . I don't know . . . eight? Or at least until she's out of the world's cutest terrorist phase?"

As they laughed together, her phone pinged again. This time, it *was* Conner. Instantly she filled with giddiness. All million and one butterflies in her stomach fluttered to life, whisking her off to Cloud Nine. It felt so good to feel happy without waiting for the other shoe to drop. Was this what love was supposed to be like?

"Look at you light up like the Christmas tree in Rockefeller Center. What does Romeo have to say?"

"He's taking me fishing tonight."

"Of everything you've said over this lunch, that one is the most unbelievable. Unless you're watching a pond on a flatscreen from the comfort of his couch. Or, like, a TV show *about* fishing. Maybe then I'd believe it." Haylee handed her card to Willamina. "You? Fishing?"

"It's part of this turning a new leaf thing."

"No, I'm pretty sure this is part of a falling in love thing."

Because denying it just might be a lie, she didn't.

Chapter Twelve

CONNER

"Are you sure you don't want to borrow my fishing poles?" Edith insisted from her side of the backyard fence as Boomer ran zoomies. She'd already handed over a picnic basket filled with goodies for his date tonight. Chicken salad sandwiches, the best chips on the planet—Edith's words—and homemade caramel brownies. And that was just what he'd seen before she closed the lid on him. "I have everything you need except fresh bait. Well, and the licenses. Suppose you'll have to stop by Evans' Outfitters for those."

"I don't want to inconvenience you."

"Honestly, my old poles need some love. They don't get out much anymore."

He liked the idea of having their own poles, but it might be wise to make sure they actually enjoyed the activity before investing a bunch of money in it. "Okay, you twisted my arm."

"Thought you might say that. Everything you need's outside my front door." She reached over the fence to rub Boomer behind the ears when he assumed the position. She looked the pup in his big brown puppy-dog eyes and said, "Now, don't capsize the boat." A sparkle danced in her eyes. "Or do. That can be romantic too."

Conner thanked her once more before she went inside, promising she'd make their Sunday evening walk. He hadn't felt this good in . . . well, ever if he was being honest. Though he had some pleasant enough memories with Veronica if he fought not to let her true character taint them, he'd never felt this way with her. Hadn't realized he *could* feel this way until he finally let his walls drop with Sadie. It was like having the world at his fingertips, even if he still felt like a nervous schoolkid getting ready to pick up his crush for the prom.

"Let's get loaded, buddy."

Boomer bolted to the door, whining as if Conner wasn't moving fast enough.

Sadie agreed to meet him at Evans' Outfitters so they could get fishing licenses. It was only through a Google search and a quick conversation with Edith that he had any idea *what* they could fish for tonight. Edith mentioned sockeye salmon, right before she hinted that they might not get all that much fishing in.

He thought it was because of it being so late.

Now, he knew better.

When he spotted Sadie behind the front counter, helping a customer check out, his entire body hummed with happiness. Or was it . . . more? It seemed too early to have fallen in love with her. Unless the feeling had been building all these months during Evans family dinners and run-ins in town that no longer felt so coincidental when he thought about it.

"Hey," she greeted with a cute wave as the customer walked off. "You ready to get some fishing licenses?"

"Sign us up."

She pulled out a binder. "I have to be honest about something," Sadie said as they each filled out their information on separate cards.

"What's that?"

"I haven't been fishing since I was eleven. And I was terrible at it. So terrible in fact that my dad refused to ever take me again."

"That's not true," Jerry Evans said, approaching them from behind the counter and dropping a hand on Sadie's shoulder. Conner stiffened, wondering if he should've approached this date differently. Was Jerry old fashioned when it came to these things? Would he disapprove simply because Sadie and Marc had their differences? "You refused to come out again because the fish were too slimy."

"Okay, that's probably true," Sadie admitted. She looked at Conner, her eyes still sparkling. Not a trace of worry about her dad being in audience. "I can't promise I won't have a repeat experience tonight."

"You can count on it," Jerry teased.

"Thanks, Dad!"

"Got everything you need?" Jerry asked Conner.

"Everything but bait."

"We're fishing for sockeyes," Sadie told her dad.

"Ah, then you'll want some bright-red lures. Come with me. I'll show you where they're at."

Conner wasn't naïve, and if he was, the apologetic look on Sadie's face would've clued him in. It felt so strange to be having a conversation like this at thirty-two years old. Conner paid attention to Jerry's instructions about the lures and what he needed to do if he wanted to actually catch something, all the while waiting for the inevitable.

When Jerry handed the package of lures to Conner, he held on until he had his attention. "I know Sadie's an adult, but she's still my little girl. She's been through a lot."

"I have nothing but respect for her," Conner said without missing a beat. Unable to keep his gaze from flickering toward the checkout counter at the fiery redhead who was as close to stealing his heart as any woman ever had been. "That's how I'll treat her."

"Good." Jerry clapped him hard on the shoulder. "Knew you would. Just had to be said. I'll be at home cleaning my shotguns tonight. You know, in case you get bored and want to see them." He winked at Conner as he cackled.

"Sadie's a lot of amazing things," Conner dared to add, pausing to ensure Jerry was really listening because what he had to say was important. "She's incredibly smart. Has a brilliant mind. But she dismisses herself too easily. She has some ideas about the store, but she's too shy to share them with you. You should ask her about them sometime. Hear her out."

Jerry seemed taken by surprise at this news, his eyebrows drawing in thoughtfully. He answered with a single nod before he was pulled away by a customer. Conner hoped it would be enough to at least start that conversation. Sadie might be a little miffed with at him at first, but he hoped it'd be worth it.

"Guess this is what we need for tonight." He held up red lures when he returned to the counter, unable to keep his eyes off the beautiful woman behind it. Her red locks were pulled into a carefree bun with a couple of spiral curls dancing near her ears. She wore the softest shade of pink lipstick, and he looked forward to messing it up later.

"Should I get any snacks?"

"Edith has us covered."

"Oh, wow. That was kind of her."

"She even packed some peanut butter dog biscuits from The Forget Me Not for Boomer. You don't mind if he comes along, right?"

"I'd be upset if you left him at home."

"Hopefully you still feel the same if he capsizes the boat."

Sadie's eyes widened in surprise. "We have a boat? I've never been fishing in an actual boat before."

SADIE

"Scratch the boat," Conner said, rubbing the back of his neck as they both stared down at the rickety structure barely floating beside the dock. If it stayed this close to shore, it wouldn't fill with enough water to sink. But they certainly couldn't take it out on the river without ending up at the bottom of it.

"It's okay," Sadie said, refusing to feel an ounce of disappointment. After all, this setting despite it being in the wilderness and a prime spot for bear sightings, was gorgeous. Straight out of a romantic movie. Well, with some imagination and a few touches, it could be a movie-worthy scene.

She pressed both hands into his bicep, and nearly forgot her name. Was it made of pure steel? How was she in the outdoors with a man who should be so far out of her league it was laughable? How was she *this* happy? How was this real life? The answers, she realized, were safest left a mystery. "We can fish from the end of the dock."

"I didn't bring any chairs."

"I brought a blanket. That's all we need." Boomer nudged her thigh with his pushy nose. "Yes, Boomer. It's big enough for all three of us."

The sun gave way to the horizon as they carried everything to the end of the dock. She spread a dark blue and green striped blanket she'd pilfered from Dad's camping tote and spread it out for everyone to sit comfortably. She'd planned to use it to keep her warm, but she had Conner for that.

He laid two poles, extra line, and lures off to one side. And a picnic basket large enough to feed her whole family behind where they'd sit. It was already perfect, but the two battery-powered candles he positioned beside the basket made her heart melt the rest of the way. He scanned the arrangement, but seemed too hesitant to sit. "I should've brought you flowers."

"Conner, it's perfect. Just like this." She reached for his cheek and tugged his face down. She had to lift on tiptoes to meet his lips in her practical shoes, but it was worth it. She didn't need her wedge sandals causing her to topple into the water. It might be romantic to be rescued, but the Alaskan water was way too frigid for her to want to test out that theory.

He kissed her softly. Thoroughly. Her toes curled, just like the heroines in romantic comedies always claimed they did. When he broke apart the kiss, she was breathless. Dizzy. From the looks of it, he was, too.

"You're a pretty great kisser," she said.

"You're pretty great yourself."

She kissed him again, just to test the theory.

She could so easily get lost in him. The thought should frighten her. Get those flight instincts kicked into overdrive. After her toxic relationship where one day things were amazing and the next they were a nightmare, what she was building with Conner should leave her feeling edgy and afraid it would all implode at any second.

Instead, all she felt was peace.

Peace she'd never experienced in her twenty-six, going on twenty-seven, years. It was as if her soul recognized his and knew it was safe.

"I'm not much for flowers," she admitted before she gave in to the urge to kiss him a third time. She wanted a peek into the picnic basket before she could be distracted by those dangerously tempting lips again. "I have a hard enough time keeping my personal relationships in check. Flowers in my hands would probably die a horrible, neglected death."

"I don't think you give yourself enough credit, Sadie. You're more resilient than you know. And you go out of your way to make people feel appreciated. Maybe that wasn't Old Sadie. But it's definitely New Sadie." The compliment warmed her from the inside out. She'd never felt so seen before. Not by anyone she'd dated, not by her friends, not by her family.

Conner led her by the hand to their picnic setup at the end of the dock. Boomer whined as he waited for them to make a spot for him. Or maybe it was his eagerness to stick his nose in the picnic basket to find those peanut butter treats.

"Fishing or dinner first?" Conner asked.

"Oh, definitely dinner. We can't start fishing until it's actually midnight, right?"

"Right. And good answer, because I'm starving."

Conner unpacked the meal Edith prepared for them, and they ate in comfortable silence as dusk fell around them, giving the wood-lined river both a magical and peaceful overlay. At the edge of the dock with feet dangling a few inches above the rushing water, Sadie didn't worry about bears or unwanted company.

She felt safe, but most of all, she felt calm.

"I posted another video of Boomer today,"

Conner said as he held out a treat for the pup and made him *take it nice*.

"The one with the carrot sticks. I saw." She rested her head on his shoulder because she could. He finished his sandwich and wrapped an arm around her, tugging her closer. Boomer wedged his nose in the small gap between their hips, but after deciding his big head wouldn't fit, groaned and lay behind them. His massive, warm body butted up to Sadie's back like a heated blanket.

"Some brand of dog toys reached out to me. Asked if I'd product test a couple of things and post the videos." He gently caressed her shoulder, making her melt with each stroke. "I'll need some help."

"You know I'll help. I'm not going anywhere."

"Good. I'd miss you."

"Did I tell you I got the apartment?"

"Really? That's great news!" He kissed her temple before resting his chin against it. "You still going to get a dog?"

"Only if you think Boomer would like a brother." She reached behind her and rubbed the pup's haunch. "I don't want him to feel replaced."

"I think he'd love a brother."

"Haylee's going to come with me after the festival's over Sunday. To the animal shelter. Maybe you should bring Boomer." Her heart raced at lightning speed as she awaited his response. A conversation like this was serious. It implied a future beyond a few dates. It was the closest she'd come to wearing her heart on her sleeve in a long time. A week ago, she would've laughed at anyone who tried to tell her she'd be on board with a committed relationship anytime in the next hundred years.

"I'd like that," Conner said.

"Yeah?"

"Of course. You mean a lot to me, Sadie. I want you to know that. This isn't just some fling I'll tire of. So, if you're only here for the thrill of going behind Marc's back—"

"Stop it," she teased, turning to face him. She reached for his cheek again, softly running her fingers through his beard. It needed a trim, but she hoped he didn't get around to it for a couple more days. She liked him a little scruffy. It made him look more Alaskan. "I'm breaking my resolution to stay single for a year to be here right now. My entire family will remind me of that publicly declared vow when they find out about us. It'll be an entertaining family dinner," she added with a laugh. "And you want to know a secret?"

"What's that?"

"I thought I'd be single . . . forever."

"Yeah, right."

She swallowed, because talking about this made her feel vulnerable. "I mean it. After Aaron . . . he messed me up in ways I can't even explain. Played all these mind games. He made me cry hysterically over the stupidest thing and then the next day, acted like the fight never happened. Acted like we were this perfect couple who was so in love. I can't tell you how many times I thought I was going crazy. But it was all him and his narcissistic need to control everything, especially me. I never wanted to risk going through that again."

"He never deserved you, Sadie." The firmness in Conner's voice bordered on protective. It held a possessive edge that gave her a slight thrill. Made her long for a real future together. She could handle this for the rest of her life, couldn't she?

"I don't exactly have a great track record when it comes to dating," she added. "It's still a little hard to believe I stumbled across a unicorn who notices me."

"A unicorn? You can't come up with something a little more manly?"

"Hey, they're majestic creatures." She gave him a quick, soft kiss. Mostly because she could. "It's a compliment, so just take it, okay?"

"Okay." He kissed her this time, not so softly. Not so quick. When he pulled back, she was dizzy in the best way. "I more than notice you, Sadie Evans. I think about you. All the time. I don't know exactly when it happened, but once I started to fall for you, there was nothing I could do to stop it. It's too late for you not to break my heart, so I really hope you don't."

"That's the last thing I plan to do, Conner."

"Good. Because you hold it in the palm of your hands."

Be still her beating heart. Her bones melted at his words, sealed with another toe-curling kiss. Would they even get to fishing tonight? She didn't care if they did. She snaked a hand around his neck to pull him closer and sank into his deepening kiss. If she wasn't in love with Conner before, she certainly was now.

Chapter Thirteen

CONNER

"I already regret this," Marc grumbled as he stood in the huddle of Sunset Ridge's bachelors awaiting their briefing. He folded his arms over his chest to emphasize his grumpiness, as if it weren't already exuding off him in waves. Conner wasn't any more thrilled about this whole arrangement, but he kept that to himself.

"It's for charity," he offered instead.

"I could just write a check. Or volunteer more hours." Marc looked over at him. "You any good with power tools? We could bail on this right now and head to the shelter to start those renovations ourselves. How's *that* for charity work?"

A loud, piercing whistle ended their conversation and drew everyone's attention to the woman standing on a metal chair to the side of the stage. Conner recognized Dani as one of the main volunteers who helped run the shelter. She was sweet and motherly to both the animals and volunteers alike. When he told her he signed up for this, she nearly started crying.

Which was the same reaction his mom and sister both had. Except, they *had* cried.

He wanted to tell them about Sadie, but he was saving that special announcement for later. They'd no doubt be so happy to hear he moved on from Veronica and didn't let her destroy his chance at happiness that they'd start planning his wedding and naming his future children. Before that onslaught happened, Sadie deserved some warning.

But he'd worry about all that after he talked to Marc man-to-man about his intentions. Which his plan as soon as they were both auctioned off to the highest bidders. Now that Sadie had officially fulfilled her commitment to the clinic, Marc couldn't hold it over her head. Conner hoped the confession wouldn't cost him a friendship, but he was too far gone when it came to Sadie. He couldn't—wouldn't—turn his back on her now. She didn't deserve that. If Marc didn't give them his blessing, Conner could only hope he'd come around down the road.

"We are ever so grateful for each and every one of you," Dani said, nearly tearing up.

Confirming he wasn't getting out of this.

Neither was Marc.

One date for charity. How bad could it be?

Though he and Sadie flirted with the idea of her bidding on him last night on the fishing dock where they proceeded not to catch any fish, they both agreed it was best not to drop a bombshell on Marc in front of half the town. Which turned out to be *most* of the town thanks to the perfect summer day. Clouds were gathering overhead, but there was no threat of rain, and the temperature was unusually warm for the coast.

He couldn't help his wandering eyes as they scanned the growing crowd. Dozens of women filed into the rows of folding chairs to take seats. Sadie was easy to spot with her red hair and bold personality. Impossible to miss, really. Which is how he knew she hadn't made it to this part of the park yet. She promised to take Boomer to the frisbee toss earlier, convinced she could teach the pup a new trick. One that was sure to go viral on Instagram.

He didn't care if Boomer had one fan or a million. He only cared that the goofy dog brought smiles and laughter to those he encountered. It seemed selfish to keep that joy all to himself.

"Everyone clear?" Dani hollered after she'd read off the simple instructions that in short amounted to: act like a charming bachelor on stage until the bidding closed and keep smiling. Marc would probably have some trouble with that one.

"Jeffrey, you're up first," Dani called to the local postmaster. "Get up there and strut your stuff."

"Yes, ma'am." He gave her a salute before taking the stage. Conner laughed at how the postmaster really seemed to get into it as the bids popped up quickly. He was about their age and in a pair of jeans instead of his usual uniform. Apparently, that combination was deadly with the ladies. They went wild with a bidding war. In only a minute, they were up to four hundred dollars.

Conner caught Marc smiling, but before he could call him out on it, he caught a ghost out of the corner of his eye. Again.

Or at least he *thought* she was a ghost.

Until the woman with long, wavy dark hair and

equally dark eyes took a seat in the third row. She caught him staring and gave him a little wave before starting a conversation with Geraldine Franks beside her. Conner's stomach plummeted to his toes at the sight of the woman who'd upended his life with her lies. Her despicable actions and heartlessness.

He hadn't heard from Detective Harlow in a few days. Hadn't considered calling her to report what he was certain were hallucinations. The thought of her poking around Sunset Ridge and stirring up trouble gave him more than enough reason to leave well enough alone. Veronica hadn't reached out during her time in town, and that stumped him. Why now? What could she possibly want from him?

"You're up, man." Marc nudged Conner. "Good luck."

"Yeah, thanks."

Conner took the stage, forcing a smile on his face. Reminding himself that it was all for a good cause. Trying to ignore the red bidding paddle in Veronica's lap. He might get lucky and end up on a date with an elderly woman, like Edith. He could handle that.

"Our next bachelor is Doctor Conner Michaelson. The thirty-two-year-old veterinarian recently relocated to Sunset Ridge this past spring from

Houston. He's a dog lover, ladies. His shepherd husky mix, Boomer, is not only a rescue—our favorite kind!—but also an Instagram sensation and heart stealer. Conner enjoys late-night walks—I didn't make that part up, I promise."

Laughter erupted in the audience, drawing his eyes to the dozen rows of seated women. He spotted Sadie in the far corner with Boomer. She gave him a flirty wave that made him forget he was supposed to be playing up his bachelor status. He missed the rest of Dani's spiel and the first few bids.

"Do I have a hundred?"

Edith raised a paddle.

He formed a heart with his fingers and held it against his chest for her, winning a few laughs from the audience.

"One twenty-five," Delilah Matthews announced, raising her paddle and causing her Yorkie to bark in her lap. He was happy to see Waffles so perky, and guess he'd laid off those cucumbers.

The bidding bounced around the audience in twenty-five-dollar increments. Mostly women with fur babies he'd treated at the clinic. Some little old ladies that made googly eyes at him. He was feeling relatively good about things until the bidding took a jump.

"Five hundred," Veronica called out, holding up her paddle. Looking smug as ever as she stared at him. As if she had a secret he desperately needed to know. The day he'd figured out she'd been stealing from the children's charity caught her off guard, left her more vulnerable than he'd ever seen her. But there wasn't a trace of that shame today. Her expression implied she was completely in charge of this situation. If she wanted to win, she would.

"Five twenty-five," Beth Evans called out from the middle of the audience.

He barely had time to flash Beth a smile of gratitude before Veronica coolly raised her paddle. "One thousand."

"Eleven hundred." Sadie's voice rang above the crowd, surprising many. Including Boomer who let out a deep bark. But no one was more surprised than Marc, who spilled water down the front of his shirt when the bottle missed his lips. His hardened expression zeroed in on Sadie. If looks could kill, Sadie would be incinerated on the spot.

Conner stared at Sadie from the stage, hoping she read the silent question on his face. *What are you doing?*

"Two thousand."

"Twenty-five hundred."

Sadie wasn't paying attention to the stage anymore. Her narrowed, determined gaze fell on Veronica. He doubted Sadie realized who was bidding on him, but even if she'd figured it out, this was not the time to play jealous girlfriend. He loved her and her fiery passion—oh, yes, he absolutely did —but he wished more than anything he could get her to cool her jets right now. To trust that he wanted nothing to do with his ex-fiancée and would get her on her way out of town to anywhere else the second he could convince her to leave.

"*Five* thousand." The smug, victorious smile Veronica sent to Sadie was noticed by half the audience as they watched the exchange with widened eyes and heated whispers. At least five phones were recording. Another five snapping pictures. Conner could only guess the rumors that'd immediately start . to circulate.

"Five thousand going once. Five thousand going twice." He caught the determined glimmer in Sadie's eyes as she finally looked at him. He gave a discreet but firm head shake, and she lowered her paddle. But she didn't look happy about it. "Sold!"

The crowd clapped, but the cheers were

awkward at best. They were all trying to piece together what had just happened.

Conner marched off the stage, his first order of business: Veronica. He hoped to be rid of her before Marc was auctioned off so he could head off his best friend before he confronted Sadie, which he most definitely would.

"*Doctor* Conner Michaelson," Veronica said in that sultry voice she used to get what she wanted. It used to work on him. It used to work on a lot of people she cheated. She shimmied from her row and met him at the side. In her designer clothes and perfectly styled hair and makeup, he felt dread. Who had she stolen from this time? "I've missed you, babe. We have *so* much to catch up on."

"Cut the crap, Veronica."

She didn't so much as blink. "If you don't want me to cause a scene, you'll behave."

Chapter Fourteen

SADIE

Sadie watched from the back row as a gorgeous woman with dark wavy hair and a slender to-die-for body wrapped in a super expensive-looking dress Sadie would never be able to afford in her wildest dreams embraced Conner like an old friend. The winning bidder kissed him on the cheek and held on to his neck with fingers Sadie could tell from thirty feet away were perfectly manicured with bright-red polish.

Boomer let out a low growl. *Smart dog.*

"Who is that?" Haylee asked. "And how does she have five thousand dollars?"

"Good question." Except, Sadie was certain she already knew the answer considering Conner was staring at the woman like he'd seen a ghost. Why wasn't he squirming out of her grasp? She remembered how easily he talked about his past as if it no longer affected him. But what if in reality he'd pushed down his feelings instead of dealing with them?

"Sadie Evans, I have a bone to pick with you." The sound of Marylou's shrill, scolding tone wasn't unfamiliar after the week they spent together. Even yesterday, Sadie managed to accidentally hang up on two people waiting on hold and mix up a couple of patient charts for the techs that had them a little less grateful for that coffee. Both situations Marylou made a point to call her out on.

But they weren't at work. She wouldn't be coming back.

Sadie's immediate reflex was to go on the defensive, but it was an old one. An urge she could now tell to take a back seat while she confronted the issue like a reasonable, mature adult. "Marylou, what's wrong?"

"I don't know what you did to that website, but you've double booked almost every appointment for next week. I've spent *all* day straightening it out. I was supposed to meet my daughter for the baking contest but I was stuck at the clinic and missed it."

"I'm so sorry—"

"I can't believe I have a voice after making all those calls. Do you know how many people yelled at me for *your* screwup?"

Sadie handed Boomer's leash to Haylee and pulled Marylou off to the side. "I'm sorry that happened, but I didn't do anything with—"

"What was *that*?" Marc snapped at her, appearing out of nowhere. She'd expected him to confront her after his bidding war ended, but where had he come from? One minute he was on stage forcing a smile as the bids jumped one by one. The next, he was in front of her, looking angrier than he had during the family meeting when he told her about Rebecca. "You say you're becoming a better person. You apologize and make me think you actually might surprise me. Then you deliberately defy my *one* request. In front of everyone."

She folded her arms, pretending she wasn't trembling a little in her sneakers. She'd expected Marc to be upset, but to yell at her in public? "I was trying to help him out, Marc," she hissed, lowering her voice.

"He raised five thousand dollars in case you missed that."

"I didn't see you bidding on anyone else."

"I'm your sister. I'm not going to bid on *you*. That would be weird."

"Yeah, a little," Marylou muttered.

"I asked you for *one* thing. To leave Conner alone. But you couldn't do that, could you?"

Sadie's heart pounded against her rib cage as she wondered if her jealous gesture meant only to save the man she was falling in love with from a nasty date was perhaps made out of fear. Fear of losing Conner. Another stolen glance at the two in deep discussion left her more uncertain of things than ever. She was already too deep. Too deep to get out without her heart taking a beating it wasn't ready for. Not when it hadn't fully healed.

"Why does it bother you so much?" she pressed, refusing to show any signs of weakness to Marc.

"Because you mess up everything you touch. Conner deserves better than for you to rip through his life like a hurricane."

"Marc, that's a little harsh—"

He turned his steely gaze on Marylou. "Did you or did you not spend all afternoon calling every single patient the website double booked? All thirty-two of them?" When he shot those laser beams for eyes at Sadie, she felt his anger boring into her. Her heart raced in warning. "You were only supposed to update the staff page. I had to call tech support on a Saturday to fix the mess you made. I'll be sending you the bill."

Sadie's entire chest buzzed uncomfortably. An anxiety attack on the verge. One she had little hope to stop. She balled her fists at her sides as her throat tightened with the tension so thick in the air she nearly choked. She desperately needed to get away from all the yelling so she could calm down. Or at least have the inevitable panic attack in peace. She would *not* give Marc the satisfaction of seeing her at her weakest.

"At least I try to fix my mistakes," she shot at him through gritted teeth.

"What's that supposed to mean?"

"Rebecca. I found her."

Marylou, obviously sensing she didn't belong in this intimate conversation anymore, slipped away.

All the anger dropped from Marc's expression, replaced by a mixture of dread and sorrow. Not the reaction she'd expected. Though, Rebecca hadn't exactly responded to her either. "Please tell me you didn't."

"She didn't answer me, if—"

"You've crossed a line. We're done, Sadie."

"Done?"

"I'm disowning you."

"You can't do that. I'm your sister."

"Only by blood. But even that doesn't matter to me now. I want you gone. I don't want you interfering in any part of my life. That includes Conner. Just pack your bags and run off like you always do after you blow everything up. We'll all be better off."

The hurt was quickly rushed by fury, but before she could get out a rebuttal or publicly declare her love for Conner—which she very nearly did—she caught the gorgeous woman leaning in and whispering something no doubt seductive in Conner's ear. If he really cared about Sadie, he would've been here by now. He would've walked away from his ex so no one got confused about any of this.

Sadie bit her tongue and spun on her heel, losing the ability to keep herself in check by the second.

When Haylee jumped up from her chair, she shook her head and sent a silent plea for her to watch Boomer.

Sadie didn't know where she was going. Only that she needed space to breathe in the most desperate way. Somewhere quiet and private to have her meltdown. This one was going to be ugly. Her walk turned into a jog, then a run, then an all-out sprint. Her feet raced along the pavement that turned to gravel until she reached a deserted end of the park. One that was more thick trees than anything else on the outskirts of town. A remote area few ever came to because there was nothing to see and signs warning to stay away. The farther in the woods she went, the darker it became.

Lungs burning from overexertion, she caught the trunk of a tree with both arms to stop her forward momentum. She pushed her back against the tree and focused on her breathing.

The tears came anyway.

Hot, heavy, uncontrollable ugly tears.

Her heart hurt. If she wasn't so familiar with these stupid anxiety attacks, she might think she was having a heart attack. But no. It was just her stupid out-of-control emotions and inability to do anything right that brought her to her literal knees.

She wanted to believe that everything wasn't one giant mess, but things weren't exactly looking great for that fairytale.

As she swiped at the moisture on her cheeks with the back of her hand, her phone pinged. No doubt Conner wondering where she'd run off to.

Or Haylee wanting to know what to do with Boomer. Or any number of people who were expecting answers she didn't have the bandwidth to give. She yearned to be her old selfish self. To lean into that flight instinct. Get in the car and head north without telling anyone she was leaving. She envied Old Sadie who could just disappear and pretend like no one cared. Old Sadie had it so much easier.

Her phone pinged again, reminding her she'd ignored the text. She considered throwing it into a marshy stream. Who needed phones anyway? But when she caught a glimpse of the text on her screen, her hands began to tremble violently.

Unknown: I'm here, Love Bug.

Sadie searched around the deserted area, gasping at every little movement and noise as her panic shot right up. No way Aaron was *right* here. Him being in Sunset Ridge was unbelievable enough. But here? At the festival? Or in the dark woods surrounding her? Not a chance.

Unless he saw her running away from everyone.

She hadn't exactly slipped away without turning heads and causing concerned murmurers. They probably thought she was hiding from the humiliation of the bidding war gone wrong.

If Aaron was in the park . . .

"No," she muttered. "He can't be."

If she just snuck back through town through less-traveled residential streets, she could lock herself in her parents' basement for a few days. Aaron wouldn't have the audacity to show up there. No one would welcome him. In fact, Dad might wave a shotgun in his face and even fire a warning shot in the air.

The image allowed Sadie the briefest smile.

It also helped her gather her wits enough to function. She slipped her phone back in her pocket, forced herself through three deep inhales and exhales, and identified a direct path to the residential area. And did her best not to panic at the growing darkness caused by an overcast sky.

If Aaron was idiotic enough to show his face in Sunset Ridge, it was because he was in his unhinged state. A side she was unfortunately too familiar with but had kept secret from everyone she knew. She thought she was protecting him, but really, she'd only endangered herself.

She made it ten steps before she screamed.

Ed marched into her path, as if he were

purposely blocking her escape, appearing twice the size as when he backed her up against her parents' house. She flattened her back against a tree, wishing she had the ability to camouflage herself from him. Was the moose out to get her or what?

"If this is about your moose wife, I already apologized." But the humor didn't do much for either of them. Sadie felt her stomach twist in anxious knots as Ed snorted several times, digging his front hoof into the ground.

This was it.

This was how it ended.

Sadie blew everything up, and as punishment, Ed was about to flatten her like a pancake. Or toss her around like a rag doll with those enormous antlers. Neither scenario gave her much hope for survival.

There was nowhere to run.

What irony.

"*There* you are." The voice from her past chilled her to the bone. She wanted to believe she was imagining it, set off by the text message and fear of dying. Aaron was clapping as he moved around a tree. "What a performance you put on, Love Bug."

"Don't. Call. Me. That."

Ed's ears were pinned all the back as he smacked

his lips. In the dusk she could see the bright whites of his eyes. All signs she'd been taught in grade school that indicated a potential attack. But as he moved, it wasn't Sadie he was pointed at; it was Aaron.

This time, it was Aaron who screamed as Ed shook the ground with his powerful charge.

Chapter Fifteen

CONNER

Fifteen minutes earlier

"Veronica, we're done here. There's a detective on the hunt for you. She knows you're here."

"You mean *Detective Harlow*?" The way she changed her voice when she spoke the name gave Conner chills. How had he not known it was her this whole time? They'd had two conversations on the phone. Two full exchanges that should've been enough to tip him off. "I guess I forgot to mention my side hustle: acting. And let's face it. You're too kind-hearted to call the police on me. It's that determination of yours to see the best in people. It's your greatest weakness."

"What are you doing here?"

"What do you think?" She snaked a hand around his neck and pulled her cheek against his to speak against his ear. "I'm a little short on cash. Oh, you'll spot me for the winning bid, right?"

"You need to leave."

"Actually, you need to write me a check unless you want me to cause problems."

"What are you talking about?"

"You should've turned me in when you had the chance. I stole way more than twenty-five grand, babe." She kissed him on the cheek, no doubt leaving behind a smear of gaudy red lipstick. He immediately glanced at the opposite end of the audience to Sadie, hoping to catch her eye. To let her know this wasn't what it no doubt looked like. But until he could be sure Veronica wasn't going to stir up actual trouble, he had to stay put.

Even as he watched Marc exit the stage after Edith won the bid and march over to Sadie. He expected the confrontation, but not until *after* the auction was over. They still had three more bachelors to flaunt. He hated leaving Sadie to deal with Marc on her own, but she was tough. So much tougher than she realized. She could handle him for a few minutes until he got there.

"And guess what?" Veronica said, turning his cheek with the sharp red nail of her index finger. "I'm taking you down with me. *Unless* you help me out. I need to get out of the country for a bit, but I can't do it on an empty bank account. Let's say fifty?"

"Fifty what?"

"Thousand."

Conner nearly choked. "You're insane."

Veronica shrugged as she followed his gaze to Sadie. "Maybe I am. But it would be a shame to be locked behind bars. Your little girlfriend might get tired of waiting for you to serve twenty years and run off with someone *not* in prison."

Conner felt sick, but that didn't mean he was giving in to any of this. He'd donate the five grand to the animal shelter because he would've done it anyway. But he wasn't giving Veronica a dime. First chance he got, he was going straight to Ryder Grant. The police chief would know how to deal with this. "Go ahead," he said to her, calling what he suspected was a bluff. But even if it wasn't, he was done having his act of misguided kindness held over his head. As he watched Sadie start to run away from the park, he lost what was left of his patience. "Do your worst. I *dare* you."

She grabbed his arm when he went to leave. "Give me the money, Conner."

"If you have anything left to say, you can say it to my lawyer." He pointed to the older man in glasses standing behind the rows of folding chairs. "Mr. Jenkins is right over there." Leaving Veronica, he hurried through the crowd to Marc, hoping he wasn't too late to fix whatever had gone down in the time his ex wasted.

"Where did she go?" Conner demanded.

"Don't know. Don't care. I'm done with her," Marc growled. "*Done.*"

It took a lot of restraint for Conner not to slug his best friend. Maybe a tooth knocked loose or a broken nose would get his attention. Or at least give him pause before he said something else he'd end up regretting. "You let her run off."

"She's a big girl. Or didn't she tell you?"

"She's your sister."

"Not anymore. If you know what's good for you—"

"Shut up."

Marc flinched as if he'd been slapped. Before he could say something that Conner would no doubt punch him for, he decided to be direct, even if Sadie hated him for it later. Finding her was more important than irritating his best friend or worrying about possible jail time for something he didn't do. Sadie was all that mattered. "She has anxiety attacks. Debilitating ones. Set off by stress. She shouldn't be alone right now."

Marc's hard expression softened. "I—I didn't know that."

"Of course, you didn't. Because, despite what you may think about her, you don't really know your sister. She puts up a tough front, but she's more fragile than she lets anyone see."

"Except you, obviously," Marc muttered.

"Because I don't judge her for her past. I don't judge her at all."

Marc looked uncomfortable as he shifted his weight from one foot to the other, staring at the ground.

"Did you know her ex has been bothering her again?" Conner was probably going to pay for that, but he didn't care. Marc needed to know what was at stake here. "He keeps changing his phone number so he can text her after she's blocked the number before it. She wants to change her phone number but doesn't want to explain to you or anyone else *why*. If

I knew who the guy was, I'd go handle the problem myself."

"What's the deal with some text messages?"

"C'mon, Marc. Do you *know* about this guy? What he's done to your sister? Get your head out of your—"

"He's right, Marc." Cody Evans stepped into their conversation, his presence surprising but instantly calming. He had that way about him. "All those times I went to Anchorage to rescue Sadie? It was from him. And before you ask why she didn't just leave him, just know it's never that simple. Stop judging her and start listening—"

A scream rang out from the wooded area now shrouded in darkness from the overcast evening sky. A shrill, high-pitched scream that made Conner's blood run cold. He didn't wait for anyone else to join him. He sprinted through the crowd with one intention: get to Sadie *now*.

Conner heard footsteps catch up to him on the pavement, both Evans brothers flanking him. The three raced toward the dark, wooded area with more than one sign warning people away. He didn't think as he ran right into the uncertainty.

Two steps in, he heard another scream. But this one wasn't Sadie's.

"Sadie?" he called out.

"Conner?"

He spotted her plastered against a tree half a second before he saw the biggest bull moose he'd ever encountered in his life charging nearby. The beast wasn't after Sadie or any of them. But some dark shadow hightailing it in the opposite direction.

Conner rushed to Sadie and pulled her into his arms. She clung to him so fiercely it caused him physical pain, but he didn't dare loosen his grip. If the moose changed course, he would take the brunt of the beating. Keeping Sadie safe was all that mattered.

"Aaron, you better hope that moose gets to you before I do," Cody yelled, sounding scarier than Conner would've expected he could. He was the easygoing Evans sibling who never seemed to let anything upset him. Until this moment, Conner didn't think Cody capable of instilling fear in anyone. He was glad to be wrong about that.

"Call him off! Call him off!" Aaron cried, running toward them as he wove through trees.

Conner clung tighter to Sadie to keep her safe. To send a message to her pathetic ex that Sadie would always have his protection.

"I need to have a few words with you." Marc's

grizzly bear timbre surprised both him and Sadie, her expression proof enough.

"Who are *you*?" Aaron grabbed a trunk and hid behind it as the moose Conner could only assume was Ed turned and trotted to a stop. No doubt debating charging again since he was still looking at them.

"I'm her oldest brother."

Despite the tenseness of the situation, Conner caught the slightest smile on Sadie's tear-streaked face. She closed her eyes and breathed a tiny sigh of relief, pressing her cheek against his shirt.

"Are you harassing her?" Marc demanded.

"No!"

"Try again," Cody barked. "Try the truth this time. Or I'll sic Ed on you."

"Who's Ed?" A few loud snorts were all it took to get that message across. "You named a moose? You people are crazy. You can't control him. He's a wild animal."

"You're right. We *can't* control him," Marc said. "So good luck. Maybe he'll go easy on you. Only break half your ribs when he stomps on you. Maybe he'll break them all. Like you said, we can't control what he does with you."

"You guys are nuts," Aaron muttered.

From behind the tree he held Sadie against, Conner watched as Cody nodded at Marc. The two stepped back in sync as Cody let out a whistle. Whether it was a pure coincidence, a miracle, or magic, Conner would never know. If he hadn't witnessed it with his own eyes, he never would've believed that Ed barreled forward as if on command, moving so fast the wind lifted Sadie's hair around her shoulders. Aaron let out a horrid screech as he took off.

Ed skidded to a stop at the curb and snorted as a dirt cloud lifted into the air around him. Making the beast appear even more majestic than he already did. Aaron ran down the street and Ed stood tall, as if daring him to come back.

"I really thought that moose had it out for me," Sadie said with a shaky laugh.

"I'd say he had your back." Conner kissed her forehead and pulled her in for a hug, never wanting to let her go. Hoping he never had to.

Chapter Sixteen

SADIE

Nothing felt better than being in Conner's embrace.

Although Boomer hugs were a close second.

Focus, Sadie.

As much as Sadie wanted to stay right here in this moment forever, reality was unavoidable. She wriggled free from his arms and put space between them so she wouldn't be tempted to do something foolish. Like kiss him. Oh, how she really wanted to kiss him. Just one last time.

But Marc was right.

Sooner or later, her train wreck of a life would wreak havoc on his. If only she'd never gotten involved with Aaron, no one would've been in danger tonight. Ed could've targeted any one of them. Hurt her brothers. Hurt Conner. All because they'd come after her when she didn't deserve saving.

"Are you okay?" Cody asked, touching her shoulder.

She pounced at him, hugging him so tightly she was probably suffocating him. "I didn't know you were going to be home for the festival."

"Jenna was homesick. I was too." Cody peeled her arms from around his neck. "We'll catch up later. I need to find Ryder. A police escort out of town might get the message across." With that, Cody took off running. Ed had sauntered off in the opposite direction after he seemed certain Aaron wouldn't be returning to bother anyone.

But that still left Marc.

"Sadie, I'm sorry."

She folded her arms over her chest, refusing to so readily accept the words she'd waited a long time to hear. *If* she accepted his apology, she wasn't going to make this easy on him. "Sorry for what exactly?"

"I didn't know. About Aaron. About your anxiety—"

"What?" She snapped her head to Conner, narrowing her eyes. She felt the betrayal like a stab to the back with the knife twisting inside. "You *told* him?"

"I had to."

"No." She shook her head. "No, you didn't."

"Sadie, it's not a big deal," Marc said.

She laughed, but not because she found any of this funny. Oh, no. She laughed at the sheer naivety in those words. "You know why I didn't want you to know, Marc? It's because now you'll always see me as someone who's fragile. Breakable. *Weak.* I could live with you thinking I was a colossal, unreliable screwup. But this?" She shook her head, wishing she could go back to this morning and stay in bed. She wouldn't start this day over. She'd hide from it. "This is so much worse."

"Sadie—"

"Don't," she said to Conner when he reached for her elbow. "I trusted you."

"You still can."

"Go back to your fiancée. You owe her a five-thousand-dollar date." Sadie snapped her attention to Marc next. "By the way, I didn't touch anything on your website that had to do with booking appointments. Whatever happened actually wasn't my fault. Not that it matters to you. You just blame me for everything that goes wrong in your life. Including

Rebecca. News flash, Marc. I didn't mess that up. You did that all on your own."

Sadie left them both and marched toward the road. She was too spent to sort all this out. Especially since she knew the best thing for everyone was her leaving town. Her heart cracked with each step she took away from Conner. Deep down, she knew he meant well. But that didn't make it okay.

Two blocks away from the festival, Sadie pulled her phone out of her back pocket to find a slew of texts from her sister.

Haylee: You okay?

Haylee: Sadie?

Haylee: Sadie???

Haylee: Did Ed get you?

Haylee: Okay, this isn't funny. Answer me!

Haylee: Please

Sadie: Bring Boomer to the house.

Haylee: Everything okay?

Sadie: Honestly? No. It's so far from okay.

Haylee: Does Conner know you want me to steal Boomer?

Sadie: It's fine.

She needed one last Boomer hug before she packed her bags. She needed to say goodbye to the one loyal friend who'd never once let her down or betrayed her secrets given in confidence. The only one who wouldn't judge her for giving in to her old ways and running.

Chapter Seventeen

SADIE

"Are you leaving?" Dad asked from her bedroom doorway as she stuffed clothes in a duffle bag. She was working hard to pack only what she needed, but she'd never been known to travel light. Which was slowing down her escape.

"I made a mess of everything. It's just . . . better this way."

Dad sat on the edge of the bed, handing her pairs of shoes she'd set aside. She'd only been able to narrow it down to six pairs, but it was an accomplishment. Maybe the only one she could feel good about. "I heard you have some ideas for the store."

Sadie stiffened, her fists balling at her sides. She'd really like to strangle Conner right now. How many of her secrets had he shared? Obviously, all of them. "Nothing important. They weren't that great anyway."

"I'd like to hear about them."

"Now?"

"You're not driving to Anchorage tonight." His stern tone reminded her of her teenage days. She'd pushed his buttons *a lot*. But he'd never budged when it mattered. "If you want to leave, you leave in the morning after you've had a good night's sleep and a balanced breakfast." He patted the mattress beside him. "You might as well tell me what your ideas are. I'm not going to leave your room until you do."

Sadie didn't have any fight left so she caved and pulled out her laptop. "Probably easier to show you, then."

Sadie woke to a screaming Melly and a full-frontal lick to the face. Her arms were wrapped around a pile of fur. Two of the sweetest eyes she'd ever seen stared up at her. "Boomer, what are you doing here?" She let out a yawn as the crying from down the hall went from ear-splitting to soft sobs. Her room was dusky, but not quite dark. Her bags were only half packed.

Groggily, she sat up in her bed, remembering how late she'd been up with Dad. Not only had he been open to her marketing ideas, he'd been excited. Something she hadn't expected in a best-case scenario where all her siblings backed her plan. He promised to adopt some of her strategies for the fall hunting season. Hinted that he wanted her on board to help. But she didn't promise what she couldn't.

When she crawled under the covers hours ago, Boomer hadn't been there.

She heard Haylee down the hall, quietly soothing Melly with her beautiful voice. She refused to sing for anyone but her daughter, and would deny she knew how if anyone complimented her abilities. One of these days, Sadie was going to catch her on camera and post it on Instagram. Except, she was leaving in a few hours and not coming back. Right.

Sadie waited for the song to end before she attempted to move Boomer off her lap.

The moment she stood, she heard a clink against her window.

She turned, and gasped.

A giant moose stared into her bedroom window. Ed was camped outside, curled in a ball that made it seem as though he always slept there. Because her room was in the lower level of the house, Ed's giant head resting on the ground was near eyelevel with Sadie. If he moved any closer, his nose would fog up the glass.

She blinked hard, certain it was some late-night hallucination, brought on by too little sleep and a super emotional evening. But when she opened them, Ed was still there. Though her pulse raced at the memory of the beast charging powerfully enough to shake the ground like an earthquake, she smiled and mouthed *thank you.*

Ed closed his eyes.

Sadie waited a moment, pondering what it might mean that Ed was here. In every matchmaking story that involved the moose, he always appeared when one of the two was ready to run. Or so the legend went. It was entirely possible that detail was embellished by the storytellers.

But could his presence be a sign? Or was it simply wishful thinking? He wasn't exactly blocking her escape like he was reported to do when someone wanted to run away as badly as she did.

Boomer groaned and stretched on her bed.

If only she had her phone. *This* was an Instagram-worthy moment if ever there was one. The thought only squeezed her heart painfully. She was going to miss them both.

She slipped quietly down the hall, stopping in the doorway of Melly's room just as Haylee laid her back in her crib. It never amazed her how mature—how much older—her little sister appeared when she was tending to her daughter. She was tired and no doubt a little cranky, but she oozed love for that little girl.

Haylee held a finger to her lips when she spotted Sadie.

In the hallway, Haylee pulled her down to the family room. "Look, I'm stupid tired," Haylee whispered. "But I need to make sure you're okay."

"I'll be okay."

"Promise me one thing."

"What?"

"Promise me you won't leave." Haylee threw her arms around Sadie's neck and suffocated her. It wasn't until Sadie heard a sniffle that she realized Haylee was crying. "You can't leave, Sadie. You can't. No way I'm letting you miss my first Taco Tuesday when I can drink margaritas with you and

Laurel. And you promised me I could sleep over in your new apartment. You can't leave."

"But Marc's right. I just make everything worse, sooner or later. It's better for everyone if I just go. Before I do something to screw up your life too."

"Marc's *not* right. Even he knows that now."

Sadie refused to acknowledge the bubble of hope that did its best to form in her chest. Marc would always see her as weak from here on out. With pity. He'd never consider her an equal. And after what she'd said about Rebecca last night, it was doubtful he wanted anything to do with her.

"I'll come visit."

"What about Conner?"

"It was just a crush."

Haylee unwrapped her arms from Sadie's neck and stared at her hard. "You're such a liar. You're in love with him. He's in love with you. New Sadie would talk to him like an adult and work this out. Don't be one of those romance novel couples that goes their separate ways all because they refuse to have one stupid conversation that could fix everything. You're better than that, Sadie."

"Is that why you kidnapped Boomer? So I'd have to talk to Conner again?"

"I didn't kidnap him. Conner brought him."

"What?"

Haylee pointed up. "He's upstairs."

Sadie's pulse doubled. No wonder Ed was camped out at her window. The tricky moose was making sure she didn't run out the back door. "Well played, Ed."

"What?"

"Nothing." She shook her head, trying to knock away the grogginess. It was too late—or too early, she really had no concept of time right now—to face Conner. As exhausted as she was, she'd certainly cave. That conversation needed a clear head. "How long has he been here?"

"All night."

It was impossible to keep every butterfly in her tummy in check when a million and one lived there. A few fluttered awake. Then a few more. "Why?"

Haylee grabbed Sadie by the shoulders and turned her toward the stairs. "If you don't get upstairs right now, I'm going to—I'm too tired to think through my threats right now. But just know you won't like it one bit. Now, go!"

Sadie went, convincing herself she only did so to prevent Haylee from crying more.

Conner was draped awkwardly across Dad's recliner that was older than Marc's ancient coffee pot. The footrest no longer stayed propped on its own. One of his legs hung over the arm of the faded blue chair, the other leg stretched straight out to the floor. He looked so uncomfortable, yet just as dreamy as the first day she laid eyes on him.

"I tried to get him to take the couch." The hushed timbre of Marc's voice startled her. He nodded toward the kitchen before she could ask what he was doing here. Because she didn't want to wake Conner, she followed him.

Marc leaned back against the kitchen counter and rubbed the sleep from his eyes. He looked worse for wear. As if he hadn't slept in days.

"No coffee?"

"It's three forty-five in the morning."

"I thought it ran through your veins black at all hours."

Marc lifted one corner of his mouth, surprising her so much she nearly tripped over her own feet. "Sometimes I drink water. Or beer." He folded his arms over his chest, but it didn't make him seem so intimidating as it usually did. "Look, I'm sorry."

"Not this again." Sadie held up her hand to stop him. "Marc, I don't want your pity."

"Pity?" He shook his head. "You'll never get pity from me."

"Then what exactly is this about?"

"I underestimated you in more ways than I can count. Conner's been trying to get me to see it all along. Long before he told me all that stuff you didn't want me to know. Which, by the way, he only told me because he was trying to find you. Trying to get it through my thick skull that it was imperative we find you before something bad happened. Which it almost did."

"That's a big fancy word for three forty-five in the morning," she teased.

"And you were right."

"Come again?" Sadie leaned closer, holding her hand over her ear. "I don't think I heard you."

Marc glared at her, letting her know exactly how uncomfortable this made him and how little patience he had for her antics. She enjoyed every second of it. "You were right. It's not your fault Rebecca left. I've been blaming you all this time so I didn't have to face the truth." Marc shifted his weight, staring at the floor. For a man who was always so certain of himself, he looked downright squirmy. "Please don't reach out to her anymore."

"But—"

"Please, Sadie. This promise I need you to keep."

She bit down on her bottom lip to keep from

saying words he clearly didn't want to hear. She didn't know enough about his history with Rebecca to help. If he wanted her to stay out of it, that's what she'd do. "I promise."

"Thank you."

"What happened to Aaron?" Sadie asked, uncertain if she wanted the answer. It was too much to hope he'd been arrested. That he might finally leave her in peace.

"Ryder caught him trying to skip town. He ran off the road and hit the town sign. Thing's steadier this time around. It didn't fall over like it did the last time it was rammed by a car. But his S10 was totaled."

"Ed," Sadie said, the thought warming her from the inside out. The moose she thought hated her was looking out for her in more ways than one.

"Sounds like he has some warrants out. He shouldn't bother you again."

"Good."

"Ryder picked up his ex, too," Marc said, nodding toward the living room. "Don't fault him for that. For not calling Ryder first thing. I've known Conner a long time. He thinks everyone deserves a chance to do the right thing. His greatest fault is that he sees the best in everyone. Even those who don't deserve it."

"It's also his best quality," Sadie pointed out.

"That it is. Now, you better go wake that poor man up," Marc said with a nod toward the living room. "He's going to have aches he never thought possible if he sleeps in that old thing any longer."

"You're okay with this? Conner and me?"

"I couldn't imagine anyone better for my little sister."

A beaming smile stretched her cheeks as she pounced, attacking him with a bear hug. Marc stayed stiff except for an awkward pat on the back. No matter. They could work on that. "I won't ruin his life. I promise I won't."

"I know you won't. I was wrong to say otherwise."

Sadie looked up at him suspiciously. "Are you a clone? Like Marc's *good* twin?"

"Knock it off." He nudged her in the direction of the living room. "Go, save the poor man from Dad's ancient recliner." She made it two steps before he said, "Sadie?"

"Yeah?"

"I don't think you're weak."

"Yeah, right."

"I think you're incredibly brave."

Her heart swelled to three times its normal size at the words she never thought she'd hear from her oldest brother. Not if they lived to be a hundred. The genuine, albeit tired, look in his eyes promised he meant them.

Chapter Eighteen

CONNER

"Conner."

Conner groaned, wondering why every single muscle in his body felt as though it was stiff and on fire at the same time. But exhaustion lulled him back to sleep, promising he could solve that unpleasant mystery later.

"Conner."

He felt his body rock from side to side until his leg suddenly dropped. He woke with a start and tumbled forward, crashing to the floor.

"Are you okay?" Sadie knelt above him, her gentle hand on his shoulder. Was he still dreaming?

He'd been camped out in the Evans' living room, hoping that eventually Boomer would coax the woman he loved from the basement. Or that he'd at least prevent her from making an escape out the back door.

"Sadie?"

"Sorry. You looked so uncomfortable. Didn't anyone warn you not to sleep in Dad's old recliner?"

"I didn't listen."

"Obviously."

He sat up and reached for her hand, fearful that if he didn't latch on to her, she'd disappear. He sat facing her. "I'm sorry," he said, knowing it was the most important thing he had to say in case she told him to go home. Well, *almost* the most important thing. But he was saving those three words until he knew they wouldn't send her running.

"I was really hurt at first," Sadie said.

"I shouldn't have told Marc—"

"No, *I* should've told my brother the truth a long time ago. You were only doing what you thought was necessary. And if you hadn't, who knows what might've happened—"

"Hey." Conner cupped her cheek and tilted her face up until she looked at him. "No what ifs, okay?

Not about this. What ifs should be saved for positive things."

"Like?"

"What if I took you midnight fishing again? Do you think we'd actually catch something this time?"

Sadie let out a carefree laugh that eased away all the tension he'd been holding since she left him in the woods. "Doubtful. We seem to get . . . distracted." The cutest blush flushed her cheeks, suggesting she was remembering their romantic evening on the dock as well.

"You're probably right."

He caressed her cheek with his thumb, resisting the urge to kiss her only because he had to be certain of one thing first. "Please stay, Sadie. Please don't run away. No matter what you might think, you're the best thing that's ever happened to me."

Boomer chose that moment to make his appearance, announcing his arrival with a groan before he plopped down across both their laps to remind them it was too early to be awake.

"Okay, *one* of the best things."

"I'm not leaving."

"You're not?"

"I mean, I was dead set on it until about half an hour ago. I didn't realize so many people in this house actually liked me." She offered him a playful smile.

"They more than like you. They love you. *I* love you."

Sadie stared at him in shock, her eyes instantly turning shiny. "You don't mean that," she said in a whisper.

"Of course, I mean it." He rested his forehead against hers. "I love you, Sadie. Maybe it only feels like a week, but I think my feelings were growing beneath the surface since the first day I met you. Of everyone at the dinner table—and it was a full house that night—you were the one I remembered the best. Your brilliant smile that lit up the room. Your clever wit and love of mashed potatoes."

"Only when Mom makes them. Because she measures the butter—"

"With her heart." That won him a bright smile that warmed him from the inside out.

"I had a crush on you since that first night," Sadie admitted. "I didn't want to. I fought it hard. But you know what?"

"What?"

"It's the best battle I've ever lost. Because if I'd won, I never would've fallen in love with you."

He drew her lips to his, melting into her kiss. A

kiss that until moments ago he wasn't certain he'd ever taste again. She combed her fingers through his beard as he deepened the kiss. Boomer grumbled below them, clearly annoyed that they weren't sleeping like he wanted to be. They shared a laugh and both rubbed the pup that lay between them. Still not quite fitting in their laps, even though there was two.

"You still think Boomer wants a brother?" Sadie asked.

The shepherd's tail thumped once against the floor.

"Sounds like a yes to me," Conner said before he pulled her in for another kiss.

Epilogue

MARC

Sadie's car was parked outside the animal shelter when Marc pulled into the tight parking lot, one with cracked pavement and weeds growing up from those cracks. The whole place needed a facelift, but the funds from the bachelor auction were most needed *inside* the facility. This weekend, he decided, he'd come back with a weed eater.

The happy yips of dogs greeted Marc as he headed inside the building the shelter had outgrown a couple of years ago.

"Oh good, you're here!" Dani Parsons said with an air of relief. "Daisy needs a nail trim. I don't know what voodoo magic you performed the last time, but she won't let me near those toes. She won't let *anyone* near them. She's in her usual spot." Dani pointed to the door leading to the kennels. "We have a new volunteer inbound any minute. I need to get ready for her."

Marc dropped a reassuring hand to Dani's shoulder, one that hardly reached his elbow. "I've got Daisy." He didn't let on his disappointment that the cocker spaniel had yet to be adopted. She was a lovable pup who'd make a great family dog, but if she was bored, she tended to chew everything in sight. If he was home more often, he'd adopt her himself. But Daisy needed someone who was around more than they weren't.

"Your sister's out back," Dani added as she hurried away.

Sadie, or maybe it was Conner—he couldn't remember anymore—mentioned a visit to the shelter this week to find Boomer a brother. Marc already knew which dog would be the best fit, but they'd have to come to that conclusion on their own.

He was still adjusting to his best friend and middle sister as a couple—something he never expected to accept, much less approve of. But in the past month, watching them together had opened his eyes in a big way. Deep in the recesses of his still-cold heart, he was happy for them.

He even had them over for a cookout last week, just the three of them. Conner met him at the grill that night to show Marc the ring he bought. To get his approval since Dad obviously already said yes. If Marc was having trouble seeing his sister as a responsible, grown woman, the two-carat diamond his best friend bought for her certainly helped adjust his perspective. If Sadie could turn a new leaf despite all the hard times he'd given her along the way, the least he could do was try to embrace this new normal.

Their blossoming relationship reminded him of happier times. But any nostalgia from his memories with Rebecca faded quickly now that he'd spent more time confronting what he'd been burying. The red flags he'd ignored from day one.

Rebecca gave Marc an ultimatum more than three years ago, but all he remembered about it was the loss. Missing her by minutes. Wondering what might have been if only Sadie had managed to stall her. For years, he unfairly blamed his sister for what he painfully came to realize was his own subconsciously purposeful failure. He sabotaged his chance, but until now, he never understood why.

Rebecca resented how busy he was. How much

time he spent at the clinic and invested in the animal shelter. How he'd leave in the middle of dinner if there was an emergency. That day when she told him to meet her on the pier or else, he had to make a choice. Sure, the pittie with the torn ACL needed surgery, but it wasn't a life-or-death situation. He didn't have to drop everything the instant the phone call came in.

But he did.

Even knowing Rebecca was waiting for what might very well be the last time.

And it was.

"Marc, I didn't realize today was your day." Sadie lit up at the sight of him—something else he was still adjusting to. But he didn't squirm so much when she threw her arms around him and squeezed him in a hug. "Boomer's getting a brother! Or at least I hope he is. Today's the meet-and-greet with Bowzer."

"They'll hit it off."

Sadie squinted her eyes at him, as if studying him too closely for comfort. "Are you . . . smiling?"

"Don't get used to it," he grumbled. "I have a reputation to uphold."

Sadie playfully rolled her eyes at him as she

pulled out her phone to check the incoming chime. "Right. Grump of the Year."

Marc stole a glimpse at his sister's left hand. *No ring yet.* But his attention quickly shifted to the phone she held. That familiar unsettling feeling returning. He'd bitten his tongue many times this past month. Or maybe, more truthfully, he'd chickened out. "Hey," he said, uncertain of the right words. "Any chance—"

"No." Sadie's answer was immediate but gentle, saving him from voicing the words that were hard enough to think, much less speak. "I didn't reach out, like I promised. Not that I could if I wanted to anymore. She actually blocked me."

Marc had been furious with Sadie when she first confessed she'd reached out to his ex. But as time went on, it forced him to sort through the past. To confront everything he'd shoved way down. Like the fact that Rebecca essentially resented who he was at his core. He wasn't going to sacrifice his identity for anyone, no matter how strong his feelings might be for them. It was time to fully accept that their relationship was never meant to work. To let go once and for all. "That's probably for the best."

"I'm sorry—"

"Don't be." They hadn't spoken much about this

since the night Conner passed out in Dad's uncomfortable recliner, hoping he hadn't lost Sadie. It was that night that Marc finally grasped the meaning of love. The *true* meaning. Conner's devotion taught him a thing or two when he was convinced he already knew it all. He and Rebecca never had that conviction. Not really. "It's in the past now. Where it belongs."

"Are you—" Sadie studied him again, that mischievous twinkle dancing in her eyes. "Are you ready to date again?"

Before Marc could clarify that he was *not* in fact ready to date again—not now, maybe not ever— Conner joined them in the back with Boomer. The pup's loud, thundering bark saving Marc from dodging any ideas Sadie might offer when it came to eligible women in Sunset Ridge. The pup went for Sadie first, then Marc.

"Maybe you should get a cat?" Sadie suggested.

"A cat?"

"You're gone a lot. Cats are self-sufficient. Plus, a brooding, grumpy man who cuddles a cat? Practically a chick magnet."

"Good luck," Marc said to Conner, taking his cue to leave them be before things got any stranger.

"With who?" Conner asked. "The dogs or—"

"Don't even say it," Sadie cut him off, playfully tapping his arm. Before Marc could reach the door, the two were lip locked.

He left them to their moment, knowing Boomer and Bowzer would hit it off instantly. There was nothing more to do here. Not when Daisy, the drama queen that she was, needed a nail trim.

Inside, Marc heard the light hum of voices and slipped quietly into the room with the kennels. Though he could spend all day talking to animals, he had a much shorter tolerance for people. If he could finish his rounds here mostly unnoticed by the volunteers, that would be a win in his book.

"Hi!" a cheerful voice erupted, startling Marc and rocking him back a step. "You must be Dr. Evans. I'm Taylor. Taylor Hart. I'm the new volunteer. I just moved to Sunset Ridge a few days ago. Dani told me to come help you with Daisy."

When he turned, he was met immediately with an outstretched hand. Taylor stood all of five foot two, maybe three. Her megawatt smile was powerful enough to light up the town in a blackout; it was positively blinding. It nearly gave him a headache to look at it.

"When someone offers you their hand, the proper thing to do is to shake it," she added, not deterred in the least by his hesitation.

"Right. Excuse my manners." He accepted her hand, all too fascinated by the way her soft, petite fingers felt against his rough palm. He tugged his hand free two seconds later and shoved it in his lab coat pocket. "I won't need help with Daisy," he said, eager to be rid of Taylor. To distance himself from the unsettling feelings stirring inside him. Her chipper demeanor was too much today. He suspected it would be too much on *any* day. "Why don't you see if Dani needs help somewhere else?"

"She was pretty insistent I help you." Taylor leaned to one side, looking around Marc at the kennel behind him. "Is that her?" she gushed, softly clapping her hands together when her gaze landed on the pup.

"Yes."

"Daisy! You are *so* precious." Taylor slipped by Marc with ease, immediately going to the cocker spaniel's kennel and opening the gate with no regard for possible aggression or anxiety. Not that it mattered. The pup's tail swished at record-breaking speeds when Taylor greeted her like an old friend. In two seconds flat, Daisy was in Taylor's arms, licking her cheeks like it was her only mission. "You are such a lover!"

"I wish others realized that," Marc said, turning his back to the duo that was cute enough to give even the biggest sourpuss a stomachache, and searched a drawer for nail clippers. "Daisy's been here for almost six weeks. I don't get it."

"Is she a chewer?" Taylor guessed.

"You might say that. She doesn't do well when left alone for long stretches of time."

Taylor set the dog on the counter that served multiple purposes now that the lone exam room was under renovation. With any luck, it'd be finished next week so Marc could dodge chattiness during his shifts here. "May I?" she asked, holding out her hands for the clippers.

"She doesn't let anyone trim her nails but me."

Something sparkled in Taylor's eyes. If Marc had to guess, it was the possibility of a challenge. "Can I *try?*"

"Suit yourself." He let out a heavy sigh, not trying at all to hide his annoyance. He had other animals to see to today. Daisy was only his first. Wasting his time waiting on a volunteer who had good intentions but would no doubt fail in the end was not on his list. Not that much *was* on his list. Aside from occasional baseball games with the guys and family dinners, Marc didn't have much going on outside of the clinic and shelter.

Hmm. Maybe I should adopt a cat.

Marc checked his phone out of habit. Never mind that the clinic wasn't open today. "She's not going to cooperate."

"I think you're wrong."

"I know these animals better than—" Marc didn't bother finishing his sentence because Taylor clipped an entire paw's worth of nails before he could get out the words. Daisy simply tilted her head at Marc, as if to ask him what the big deal was. Daisy. The dog that made certain the entire town thought she was being murdered if anyone dared go near her precious nails.

"You know," Taylor said, moving to a rear paw, Daisy cooperating as if the two went through this routine every day. "I think *I* might adopt Daisy." With one paw to go, she stopped to cup the pup's face, leaning her own close. Daisy rewarded her with a lick to the cheek. "Would you like that, girl?"

Marc bristled. "She needs someone who's home a lot."

"I know." Taylor quickly clipped the pup's last paw's worth of nails and handed back the clippers. "I work from home. And I'm certain Dani would let me bring her to the shelter when I volunteer. It'll be perfect!"

Because Marc had no reasonable objections, he forced a smile. Judging by Taylor's confused expression, it wasn't a very convincing one. "Does your husband work from home too?"

"If you're asking me out, Dr. Evans, the answer is no." Taylor offered him a sweet smile that hinted at no malice. Only simple fact.

"I wasn't—"

"C'mon, Daisy," she said, scooping the pup into her arms. "Let's go see about adoption papers."

Marc watched the duo leave, though he pretended not to. What just happened? He wasn't asking her out. He simply wanted to know if Daisy was going to a good home. She deserved the best. It was that and nothing more.

Liar.

Sign up for Jacqueline Winter's newsletter to receive alerts about current projects and new releases!

http://eepurl.com/du18iz

Other Books by Jacqueline Winters

SWEET ROMANCE

Sunset Ridge Series
- 1 - Moose Be Love
- 2 - My Favorite Moosetake
- 3 - Annoymoosely Yours
- 4 - Love & Moosechief
- 5 - Under the Mooseltoe
- 6 - Moosely Over You
- 7 - Absomoosely in Love
- 8 - Perfectly Moosematched
- 9 - Almoose Love
- 10 - Chrismoose Kisses

Starlight Cowboys Series

1 - Cowboys & Starlight

2 - Cowboys & Firelight

3 - Cowboys & Sunrises

4 - Cowboys & Moonlight

5 - Cowboys & Mistletoe

6 - Cowboys & Shooting Stars

Christmas in Snowy Falls

1 - Pawsitively in Love Again at Christmas

2 - Pawsitively Home for Christmas

3 - Pawsitively Yours for Christmas

Stand-Alone

*Hooked on You

STEAMY ROMANTIC SUSPENSE

Willow Creek Series

1 - Sweetly Scandalous

2 - Secretly Scandalous

3 - Simply Scandalous

About the Author

Jacqueline Winters has been writing since she was nine years old when she'd sneak stacks of paper from her grandma's closet and fill them with adventure. She grew up in small-town Nebraska and spent a decade living in beautiful Alaska. She writes sweet contemporary romance and contemporary romantic suspense.

She's a sucker for happily ever after's, has a sweet tooth that can be sated with cupcakes, and is a dog mom to a lovable Alaskan Husky. On a relaxing evening, you can find her at her computer writing her next novel with her faithful dog poking his adorable nose over her keyboard, demanding treats and/or pets. Usually both.

www.ingramcontent.com/pod-product-compliance
Lightning Source LLC
Chambersburg PA
CBHW020551020726
47494CB00006B/2018